# TEN 10-MINUTE PLAYS

## VOLUME II

*Edited by*

*WALTER WYKES*

Black Box Press
Arlington, TX

Library of Congress Control Number: 2008907223

ISBN 978-0-6152-4000-8

First Edition

# CONTENTS

# WHILE THE AUTO WAITS

## O. HENRY

Adapted for the stage by Walter Wykes

*While the Auto Waits* premiered at the Fullerton College Theatre Festival in Fullerton, California, on March 16, 2007, under the direction of Kelly Newhouse. The cast was as follows:

GIRL: Alexis Brown
YOUNG MAN: David Tabarez
WAITRESS: Aida Barnes
CHAUFFEUR: Michael Segura

SETTING:
A park.

*[Twilight. The quiet corner of a city park. A GIRL in gray sits alone on a bench, reading her book. A large-meshed veil hangs over her face, which nevertheless shines through with a calm and unconscious beauty. When she turns a page, the book slips from her hand, and a YOUNG MAN, who has been hovering nearby, pounces on it. He returns it to her with a gallant and hopeful air.]*

GIRL: Oh, thank you.

YOUNG MAN: Nice weather we're having.

GIRL: Yes.
 *[Pause.]*

YOUNG MAN: Well …

GIRL: You may sit down, if you like.

YOUNG MAN: *[Eagerly.]* Are you sure? I don't want to interrupt your reading.

GIRL: Really, sit. I would like very much to have you do so. The light is too bad for reading. I would prefer to talk.

YOUNG MAN: Well, if you insist.
 *[He slides hopefully onto the seat next to her.]*
You know, you've got to be the stunningest girl I've ever seen. Honest. I had my eye on you since yesterday.

GIRL: Yesterday?

YOUNG MAN: Didn't know somebody was bowled over by those pretty lamps of yours, did you, honeysuckle?

GIRL: Whoever you are, you must remember that I am a lady. I will excuse the remark you have just made because the mistake was, doubtless, not an unnatural one—in your circle. I asked you to sit down; if the invitation must constitute me your honeysuckle, consider it withdrawn.

YOUNG MAN: Sorry.  I'm sorry.  I didn't mean to offend you.  I just thought … well, I mean, there are girls in parks, you know—that is, of course, you don't know, but—

GIRL: Abandon the subject, if you please.  Of course I know.

YOUNG MAN: Right.

GIRL: Now, tell me about these people passing and crowding, each way, along these paths.  Where are they going?  Why do they hurry so?  Are they happy?

YOUNG MAN: It is interesting to watch them—isn't it?  The wonderful drama of life.  Some are going to supper and some to— er—other places.  One can't help but wonder what their histories are.

GIRL: Yes!  How fascinating they seem to me—rushing about with their petty little dreams and their common worries!  I come here to sit because here, only, can I be near the great, common, throbbing heart of humanity.  My part in life is cast where its beating is never felt.  Can you surmise why I spoke to you, Mr.—?

YOUNG MAN: Parkenstacker.  And your name…?
    [He waits, eager and hopeful, but she only holds up a slender
    finger and smiles slightly.]

GIRL: No, you would recognize it immediately.  It is simply impossible to keep one's name out of the papers.  Or even one's portrait.  This veil and this hat—my maid's, of course—are my only protection.  They furnish me with an incog.  You should have seen the chauffeur staring when he thought I did not see.  Candidly, there are five or six names that belong in the holy of holies, and mine, by the accident of birth, is one of them.  I spoke to you, Mr. Stackenpot—

YOUNG MAN: Parkenstacker.

GIRL: —Mr. Parkenstacker, because I wanted to talk, for once, with a natural man—a real man—one unspoiled by the despicable gloss of wealth and supposed social superiority. Oh! You have no idea how weary I am of it—money, money, money! And of the men who surround me, dancing like little marionettes all cut from the same pattern. I am sick of pleasure, of jewels, of travel, of society, of luxuries of all kinds!

YOUNG MAN: I always had the idea that money must be a pretty good thing.

GIRL: A competence is to be desired, certainly. But when you have so many millions that—!
*[She concludes the sentence with a gesture of despair.]*
It is the monotony of it that palls. Drives, dinners, theatres, balls, suppers, balls, dinners, more balls, followed of course by dinners and suppers, with the gilding of superfluous wealth over it all. Sometimes the very tinkle of the ice in my champagne glass nearly drives me mad.

YOUNG MAN: You know … I've always liked to read up on the habits and customs of the wealthy class. I consider myself a bit of a connoisseur on the subject. But I like to have my information accurate. Now, I had formed the opinion that champagne is cooled in the bottle and not by placing ice in the glass.
*[The GIRL gives a musical laugh of genuine amusement.]*

GIRL: You must understand that we of the non-useful class depend for our amusement upon departure from precedent. Just now it is a fad to put ice in champagne. The idea was originated by a visiting Prince of Tartary while dining at the Waldorf. It will soon give way to some other whim. Just as, at a dinner party this week on Madison Avenue, a green kid glove was laid by the plate of each guest to be put on and used while eating olives.

YOUNG MAN: *[Humbly.]* I see.

GIRL: These special diversions of the inner circle do not become familiar to the common public, of course.

YOUNG MAN: Of course. It's all quite fascinating. I've always wanted to participate in, or at least witness first hand, the rituals of the elite.

GIRL: We are drawn to that which we do not understand.

YOUNG MAN: I guess that's true.

GIRL: For my part, I have always thought that if I should ever love a man it would be one of lowly station. One who is a worker and not a drone. But, doubtless, the claims of caste and wealth will prove stronger than my inclination. Just now I am besieged by two suitors. One is Grand Duke of a German principality. I think he has, or has had, a wife, somewhere, driven mad by his intemperance and cruelty. The other is an English Marquis, so cold and mercenary that I prefer even the diabolical nature of the Duke. What is it that impels me to tell you these things, Mr. Packenwacker?

YOUNG MAN: Parkenstacker.

GIRL: Of course.

YOUNG MAN: I don't know why you should bare your soul to a common man like me, but you can't know how much I appreciate your confidences.
> *[The girl contemplates him with the calm, impersonal regard that befits the difference in their stations.]*

GIRL: What is your line of business, if you don't mind my asking?

YOUNG MAN: A very humble one. But I hope to rise in the world someday.

GIRL: You have aspirations?

YOUNG MAN: Oh, yes. There's so much I want to do.

GIRL: I admire your enthusiasm. I, myself, can find very little to be enthused about, burdened, as I am, by the constant pleasures and diversions of my class.

YOUNG MAN: Did you really mean it, before, when you said you could love a man of lowly station?

GIRL: Indeed I did. But I said "might."

YOUNG MAN: Why only "might?"

GIRL: Well, there are the Grand Duke and the Marquis to think of, you know.

YOUNG MAN: But you've said yourself—they're so cold.

GIRL: I am sure you understand when I say there are certain expectations of a young lady in my position. It would be such a disappointment to certain members of my family if I were to marry a commoner as we like to call them. You simply cannot imagine the scandal it would cause. All the magazines would remark upon it. I might even be cut off from the family fortune. And yet … no calling could be too humble were the man I loved all that I wish him to be.

YOUNG MAN: I work in a restaurant.
    *[The girl shrinks slightly.]*

GIRL: Not as a waiter? Labor is noble, but personal attendance, you know—valets and—

YOUNG MAN: Not a waiter. I'm a cashier in … in that restaurant over there.

GIRL: *[With a strange, suspicious look.]* That … that one there?
    *[He nods.]*
*That one?*

YOUNG MAN: Yes.

GIRL: *[Confused.]* Are you sure?

YOUNG MAN: Quite sure.

GIRL: But—
> *[Suddenly the GIRL consults a tiny watch set in a bracelet of rich design upon her wrist. She rises with a start.]*

Oh!

YOUNG MAN: What is it? What's wrong?

GIRL: I ... I am late for an important engagement.

YOUNG MAN: An engagement?

GIRL: Yes!

YOUNG MAN: Some sort of ball or—

GIRL: Yes, yes!

YOUNG MAN: Will I see you again?

GIRL: I do not know. Perhaps—but the whim may not seize me again. I must go quickly now. There is a dinner, and a box at the play—and, oh! The same old round! Perhaps you noticed an automobile at the upper corner of the park as you came. One with a white body.

YOUNG MAN: *[Knitting his brow strangely.]* And red running gear?

GIRL: Yes. I always come in that. Pierre waits for me there. He supposes me to be shopping in the department store across the square. Conceive of the bondage of the life wherein we must deceive even our chauffeurs. Good-night.

YOUNG MAN: Wait! It's getting dark, and the park is full of questionable characters. Can't I walk you to your—

GIRL: *[Quickly.]* No! I mean … no. If you have the slightest regard for my wishes, you will remain on this bench for ten minutes after I have left. I do not mean to question your intentions, but you are probably aware that autos generally bear the monogram of their owner. Again, good-night.
> *[Suddenly a WAITRESS approaches, wearing a soiled, dirty uniform—evidently just coming off her shift.]*

WAITRESS: Mary-Jane! Mary-Jane Parker! What on earth are you doing out here?! Don't you know what time it is?!

GIRL: *[A little flustered.]* To whom are you speaking, Madame?

WAITRESS: To whom am I … to you! Who do you think, you ninny?!

GIRL: Then I'm sure I don't know what you're talking about.

WAITRESS: You're shift started fifteen minutes ago! Mr. Witherspoon's in a rage! This is the third time this month you've been late! You'd better get yourself over there and into uniform before he cuts you loose for good!

GIRL: I—

WAITRESS: Go on, now! I know you can't afford to miss a paycheck!

GIRL: *[Attempting to maintain her dignity.]* You must have me confused with—with someone else.

WAITRESS: Confused with—why, Mary-Jane Parker, we've known each other for three years! We swap shifts! Have you been drinking?! Why are you wearing that ridiculous hat?!

GIRL: *[To the YOUNG MAN.]* I ... I'm sorry, Mr. Porkenblogger—

YOUNG MAN: Parkenstacker.

GIRL: Parkenstacker.

WAITRESS: Parkenstacker?

YOUNG MAN: Yes, Parkenstacker.

WAITRESS: As in THE Parkenstackers?! From the society pages?!

GIRL: The society pages?

YOUNG MAN: If only I were so fortunate.

GIRL: You ... you must excuse me. My chauffeur is waiting.

WAITRESS: Chauffeur?! What kind of crazy airs are you putting on?! You've never had a chauffeur in your life! You don't even own an automobile!

GIRL: I do so!

WAITRESS: Since when?!

GIRL: Since ... Oh, get away from me! I don't know you!

WAITRESS: Don't know me?! You *have* been drinking! I'm going to tell your mother!
> *[The GIRL rushes off, followed closely by the WAITRESS. The YOUNG MAN picks up her book where she has dropped it.]*

YOUNG MAN: Wait! You forgot your—
> *[But they are gone. After a few moments, a CHAUFFEUR approaches cautiously.]*

CHAUFFEUR: Begging your pardon, sir.

YOUNG MAN: Yes, Henri?

CHAUFFEUR: I don't mean to intrude, but your dinner reservation—shall I cancel or—

YOUNG MAN: No ... I'm coming.

CHAUFFEUR: Very good, sir.  The auto is waiting.
   *[The CHAUFFEUR exits and leaves the YOUNG MAN standing alone for a moment as the lights fade.]*


\* \* \*

# SIXTY YEARS, TO LIFE

## NICK ZAGONE

Song "Sixty Years, To Life" by Heidi McIsaac

*Sixty Years, to Life* was first produced on October 30, 2007, in *Frenching the Bones: a night of nine short plays about Horror and Food* by Portland Center Stage's Playgroup at CoHo Productions. The production was directed by Matthew B. Zrebski. The cast was as follows:

GWEN: Cecily Overman

SETTING:
A prison visiting station.

*[A frame, or a piece of glass center stage, with a short counter pointed upstage to represent a prison visiting station. There's a phone receiver on the upstage side of the window as well.]*

*[GWEN enters, a little clumsily. She's carrying a guitar case, a picnic basket and a purse. She downs some Pepto and belches.]*

*[Someone's called to her.]*

GWEN: All right, all right. Can you give a girl a minute to primp? Quit rushin' me.
    *[She does the sign of the cross then crosses to the window and begins to look in it/out at us with big smile.]*
Alrighty poop-bear, are you ready for your little puppy?
    *[Smile drops.]*
Oh my goodness. Poop-bear? Honey is that you? What? Oh.
    *[picks up phone receiver]*
Poop-bear? Honey is that you? Is that him? I can barely see his little face! What did they do to you Poop-bear?

Oh now take him out of that, just take him out of that right now it's just not necessary— There's a window here for goodness sake. Where's the warden? Go get me the warden. Are they going to get the warden? Hey where are you two going? Hey!!

Oh my, poor honey. Can you hear me in there? You'd think you were that Hannibal Leck-a-ter or somethin' in that masky contraption. Honey can you blink for me? So I know you're listnin'? Poop-bear blink once if you can hear me—twice if you can't.

Well this is certainly going to be a one-way conversation. Oh I hate this phone. But I came prepared this time.
    *[She unplugs the phone and plugs in a headset.]*
What did you do hon, to get in that crazy suit? Now you didn't get violent or anything? Try not get frustrated bear, it's going to be all right I swear.
    *[She's got the headset on.]*
Now. How do I look? Can you hear me huh? Look like I'm on American Idol? Good idea huh?

So are you eating good? Huh? Keep your strength up? Did you get the food I sent? The magazines? That's good blinkin' honey were gonna be all right I think. Well I know they're workin' us over pretty good, but… I… Now I know you don't want to say anything more to get you in trouble, but I think honesty is really the best policy at this point—now don't look at me like that, they didn't tell me to say that, I had to say that 'cause…

*(sighs)* Oh honey what're we gonna do with you? With us? You really got yourself into a heap of poop this time poop bear. I know you're sorry, I know. But… You think you're so smart. It's almost as if you really believe that I didn't know.

Of course, known about it the whole time. Oh, I see that got your eyes blinkin' now didn't it. Yes, I know, I knew. A long time, well, I shouldn't say that 'cause I really don't know how long your little killing spree problem's went on, but it's been a spell. The problem now is they're askin' me a lot of questions about these girls see… But don't you worry I haven't said a word. Not a word. I'm like the Go-Go's, my lips are sealed! *(laughs)* You like that one?

But, honey pot, you should just tell them where some of them are so they can commute your sentence, that's what they said. 'Cause they told me if you tell them where you put some of those girls I could see you more. And I think we need to see more of each other. And I'm sure they'd get you out of that contraption, which is just ridiculous. They also told me that if I told them what I know they might let me even get a conjugal visit. *(laughs)* I know you told me not to talk to them and you're right, I think they're messin' with me… but I also think you should take them up on it. But you're right, ya know what, I'm going to leave that up you. And I didn't tell them anything don't worry, but you, YOU got to tell them where some of their parts are or somethin' or they're going to just treat you worse and worse. Give 'em like one of their heads, or an arm or a finger or somethin', just give 'em a hint. They already found a lot of stuff in our freezer in the basement so I don't see what the big deal is! See we should be seein' more of each other now 'cause…

Look what I brought. Surprise! A picnic! They said they'd let me
bring this in. Look! A pic-a-nic basket. Like Yogi Bear! Eh? Boo-
boo? Let me just set this up, EVEN though I know you can't eat, I just
thought it would be nice to take us back… oh, here they come. Well
of course I know he can't accept it, there's a window between us duh!
How's he supposed to eat anything in that straight jacket thing
anyway? Geez, cops sure are stupid. Oh damn I busted the crackers
—now just get back over there officer Poncherello, he ain't goin'
nowhere!

Now. So I thought we'd have a little picnic just like we did on our
first date, up in the park? Ya know, by that first girl they found, down
by the river? Well of course you remember. A little cheese, salami,
French bread, this is that good French bread, it's from Safeway. And
this is the coup de gracie.
   *[Pulls out bottle of wine.]*
Hm? It's a merlot. Like… like we used to have. Like blood huh?
That's why the Christian's drink it. 'Cause Jesus gave his blood at the
Last Supper. Cistercians and Benedictines grew grapes for wine in the
middle-ages for the mass. Yeah, I've been doing some research.
Proud of me? Now I see your eyes. No this was my idea, not the cops.

Look bear, you know, you know what they're saying? Not the papers.
Them. These detectives. Oh poop-bear… they're saying you ate those
girls. Ate them. They saw bite marks on… the bones. I told them that
it must have been a critter or somethin', a wolf, a bear or… but they
said the marks,  the in-den-ta-tions match your teeth. Now I need to
know. I need to know now. You're all I know, you're the only person
I can believe. No more secrets because…

The news is all sayin' these girls had merlot in their stomachs and
well, a heck of a lot of people drink merlot, so my boyfriend drinks
merlot, and then sometimes I wash some blood out of his shirts, but
that's from the hunting trip he says and that's what all that cured meat
in the basement is, just deer meat, venison you say, and all this
doesn't mean my boyfriend is a serial killer, it doesn't mean anything,
none of it means anything, he just has a little problem, but eating?
Eating women hon?! And don't tell me I should be happy in a way

because you didn't have sex with them, that's what one of those cops said, the little shit, but damn poop-bear I'd give anything at this point to just have a two timing philandering son-of-a-bitch. A cheater, why couldn't you just cheat hon? A DUI! Holding up an AM/PM?! Why's it gotta be eating human flesh? Why now when I'm...

*[She pops the wine, pours.]*
I know you can't speak. And knowing you, you probably wouldn't. But when you do, I want the truth. It's important now...

'Cause, I'll never escape you. Whether I stand beside you or don't. Whether you're in there five years or a hundred. You'll never leave me. I'll never not be reminded of you. You may go on in there alone without me, but out here, you're everywhere. Whether you live or die. This is my blood, I give it up for you.

Guess you would have done really well up in the Andes mountains with that soccer team. Always wondered why you bought that DVD. You're a sick, sick little poop-bear. But you're my poop bear.

*[Downs some wine.]*
Well I came here for the last time because—beyond the cops pushin' me around—I wrote a song, last night. I needed to, I don't know what else to do.

*[GWEN strums on her guitar, sings.]*

He's got... one thing on his mind
He's got... too much time to think
Three minutes to talk on the phone in the hall
He's got... four walls, a bucket, and a sink
He's got... sixty years to life
He's got... sixty years to life

We all have our problems, some have more some have less
When I met the man of my dreams, it was not a dream, to wind up in this mess
But what else do you do? You love him, he loves you
You would not run, you would not leave him this way
You would stand by him, just like I stand today

See my boyfriend, he might got himself caught up in jail
He might have killed two dozen women, give or take a few
Despite his flaws I stay with him, support him without fail
Because I love him, I know he loves me too

Now your boyfriend, he may be wearin' women's clothes
He may be sellin' your home movies on the Internet
The point I'm tryin' to make is this, we never really know
We all have secrets, some secrets we regret

He's got him, sixty years to life. Sixty years to life
I will gladly wait and I will proudly be his wife
Even if it takes, sixty years to life
        *[She crosses out from behind window, sings to audience.]*

So I will hope and I will pray. I do not know what else there is
And though it may appear that I am strong and I am sure
I have my worries. God knows he has his
But what else do you do? You love him, he loves you
I will tell him I am here for him, I will tell him I will wait
And I will tell him... that I am five days late...

They gave him, sixty years to life. Sixty years to life
Sixty years to life. Sixty years to life

I got... one thing on my mind
I got... too much time to think
Bell keeps ringing on the phone in the hall
I got... four walls, and some, wine to drink

*(beat, lights fade, out)*


END OF PLAY

# LURES

JEANETTE D. FARR

*Lures* was first produced on November 3, 2006, at the Secret Rose Theater in North Hollywood, California, under the direction of Robert Norman Knight. The cast was as follows:

BOB: Kevin McKim
MAUREEN: Meagan Johnson Briones

SETTING:
Wilderness.

*[Wilderness. A man 30—40 stands in the cold near a lake. He has a tackle box next to him, hands in his pockets. He seems either cold or nervous, we really can't tell. After a moment, a woman approaches. She is dressed like a mom – in a warm-up suit and tennis shoes. Her hair is in a ponytail – not a neat one by any means. She catches his eye. He starts to leave.]*

MAUREEN: Don't leave. On my account, I mean. I am supposed to meet someone here.

BOB: I haven't seen anyone.

MAUREEN: You waiting for someone?

BOB: Yeah… My son. He's fishing. We're fishing.

MAUREEN: Oh. A good spot, huh? To fish I mean.

BOB: That's what they say.

MAUREEN: Catch anything?

BOB: Nah. Too cold, probably.

MAUREEN: Your first time?

BOB: Fishing?

MAUREEN: Here. Fishing here.

BOB: Sure is pretty. You zone out after a while looking at it all. Not much to see anymore, it's getting dark. Nice chatting, though. So long.

MAUREEN: What about your son?

BOB: What? Oh. I'm sure he went back to the car already.

MAUREEN: The burgundy van, right?

27

BOB: Do I know you?

MAUREEN: I would think you would've gone with him. Your son.

BOB: Do you need some help finding the road?

MAUREEN: I would go places with my son. You just can't be too careful these days. The people out there.

BOB: I could go back, call someone for you.

MAUREEN: You just don't strike me as a parent.

BOB: I told you, I'm here with— Fuck it. I'm outta here.

MAUREEN: I used to think we could help you sick fuckers, that somehow pedaphilia was curable.

BOB: Look, lady, I don't know you – can you let me by?

MAUREEN: Cut the shit!
    *[She threatens him with a baseball bat.]*
Give me your shoes.

BOB: I told you, my son...

MAUREEN: You do know me. Lilpete4673. Teenspace, right? Well guess what—you thought it was him, this is what you get.

BOB: I'm here fishing—

MAUREEN: Give me your goddamned shoes!

BOB: My son went to pee, he'll be back, you'll see.

MAUREEN: What's his name? Call him.

BOB: I'm sure as hell not going to tell you anything about my son.

MAUREEN: What? You think I'm going to do something? That's a laugh. Sit down! Admit why you are here. Tell me what you were going to do.

BOB: Why are you doing this?

MAUREEN: I'm trying to get in your sick head. You're gonna tell me he is your first? Why any human being on the planet would lure innocent children to—

BOB: I was fishing!
   *[She hits him in the back with the baseball bat.]*

MAUREEN: You don't even have a fishing pole.

BOB: You have a bat, but we're not exactly playing baseball, are we?
   *[She whacks him again. Lower. His knees buckle. He's down on the ground.]*

BOB: He took it back with him. We had some things to load. He was cold.

MAUREEN: Give me your jacket. *(yelling)* NOW!

BOB: It's freez—
   *[HE complies, not sure if he's going to get whacked again. MAUREEN looks in all pockets.]*

MAUREEN: Where is it?

BOB: Where is what?

MAUREEN: What you promised me. Him. What you promised him. A baseball card. Where is it?

BOB: I don't—

MAUREEN: *(reciting)* I like to fish, maybe we could meet sometime. I told – He told you he likes baseball.

BOB: Who!?

MAUREEN: My son. Look. You thought you were talking to an eight year old, right? But it was me, instead. Your worst nightmare. A parent. You're lucky it's me and not the cops. You know what they do to you in prison. Huh? I'm not that cruel.

BOB: Please, lady. I think you broke a rib. Calm down, would ya?

MAUREEN: You told him you would bring him a vintage Babe Ruth when you met. Where the fuck is it?

BOB: You got the wrong guy, lady. I'm sorry if your son has been downloading porn or something while you're at PTA or getting your nails done. Feel guilty – fine by me – but don't you pull a Babe Ruth just because you're a bad parent and you think something's going on with me and your son –
> *[She raises the bat and gets ready to swing. He catches it and pulls her down. He puts the large end of the bat to her throat. He has the upper hand now.]*

BOB: What do you think now, huh? How do you like it, huh you crazy bitch?!

MAUREEN: My son was raped with his own baseball bat.
> *[BOB backs off, still holding on to the bat.]*
*(breaking down)* You don't talk about my son. You don't have any right to even think about my son.

BOB: *(Looking at the bat, horrified.)* Lady – I'm sorry. You got the wrong guy.

MAUREEN: Pete was only 78 pounds. A grown man versus 78 pounds. He fought like hell to get that monster offa him.

BOB: There was a person here earlier. Shady looking guy. He saw me and my son and left. Probably got spooked. Can't imagine those types would do anything with people around.
   *[Pause.]*
You okay?

MAUREEN: *(stunned)* Oh, god. I'm sorry. Are you okay?
   *[SHE approaches him, reaching out. He's spooked and pulls away quickly.]*

MAUREEN: I'm not. I'm not myself.

BOB: I'd hate to meet the real you then.
   *[MAUREEN and BOB share a nervous laugh.]*

MAUREEN: Humor. My therapist says that laughing is good. A release of chemicals.

BOB: Funny—great. Can you get me a stretcher please?

MAUREEN: Oh, god. Are you really hurt?

BOB: I'm fine. At least I think I am. Just, I don't think I'm ready to give this back yet. You know my boy has to be about the same age. In the Boy Scouts. That's why I wasn't so worried about him, you know? He's pretty good at finding his way. Likes to be independent. How old is your boy?

 MAUREEN: He was eleven when he… It first happened when he was only eight years old. After that was when the real torture began. Once was enough… enough for anyone.

BOB: You should tell someone. I could talk to him, if you want.

MAUREEN: It doesn't matter anymore.

BOB: Of course it matters. You have to.

MAUREEN: They knew. We did. Still too much for an eleven year old, thinking about girls, and dating. I couldn't even count the nightmares he had about it. Or the ones he didn't tell me about. He loved baseball. So he – *(can't bring herself to say it)* Most Moms would be pissed at their kid for ending it. I don't blame him, you know. Figured the best thing for him was to leave this world.

BOB: I'm sorry for your loss.

MAUREEN: Thank you.

BOB: You and your husband must've been mad as hell.

MAUREEN: He was overseas serving at the time. Left the anger and me in charge of dealing with it all. Paul became obsessed with e-mails, then websites, then chatrooms. Seems so impersonal to me. But he said it was the best way to make friends.

BOB: I served in the Gulf.

MAUREEN: Oh god. If I knew then…

BOB: Cut yourself some slack. I don't judge. Can't compare to what you went through.

MAUREEN: How long did you serve?

BOB: Eight months in the Marine Corps. Kids don't think of you as much of a hero these days. Not like they used to.

MAUREEN: Pete always thought his father was a hero. We just… we just couldn't get past it his father and I. Or I couldn't get past it. We just sort of grew apart after Pete… after he…

BOB: I get it. There are places, you know. To get help.

MAUREEN: Oh, shit. You think I'm going to off myself now, is that it?

BOB: It helps to talk about it, right? I'm just saying that maybe you should think about getting help.

MAUREEN: They already got me on plenty.

BOB: What's their cocktail for ya? Zoloft?

MAUREEN: Atavan. Sometimes Xanax. Helps me sleep. That's when it's the worst.

BOB: Yep. I remember. I'm off it all now. But I don't know how I would've done without it after I came back. Some guys aren't so lucky. Do worse. Stuff without a prescription.

MAUREEN: My husband wouldn't talk about what happened there or here. Let it go, he said. Forget it. He didn't think that back home things were big enough fish to fry.

BOB: Fish. Geez. My son must really be freaked by now. Can I?
    *[BOB points to the shoes.]*

MAUREEN: Oh, god. Sure. God. I'm sorry.

BOB: I told him I would watch the sunset and then we'd go. *(Putting on shoes)* You going to be okay out here?

MAUREEN: You know my Petie, he always hated when I called him Petie, but I told him it didn't matter 'cause he was my Petie—he used to like coming here. It's why I suggested it to the creep in the first place. Figured if I caught him, it might be some sort of tribute.

BOB: I'm sure he's long gone by now.

MAUREEN: Whether I catch him – or someone like him. I don't care. I think I'd feel better. Hell, I don't know. It was my therapist who suggested visiting some of the places he liked to help with the grieving process.

BOB: I hope you find the bastard that e-mailed him…you. Be careful. You could get hurt.

MAUREEN: They're cowards. Why else would they pick on children? Besides, I think I can defend myself.

BOB: I have no doubt about that. You're batting a hundred.

MAUREEN: Still sore? What am I thinking? Of course you are.

BOB: I don't judge. Besides nothing some Aspirin won't help. From Ativan to Aspirin. Hey, there's something to look forward to.

MAUREEN: You are kind, you know that? Nobody's been this kind, really.

BOB: We're human beings after all. All put here for the same thing, right?

MAUREEN: To fight like hell.

BOB: Hoo-Rah! You do have quite a swing there. You should have your own baseball card…
      *[An awkward laugh. Glad it's over.]*

MAUREEN: Maureen.

BOB: Take care of yourself, Maureen.

MAUREEN: Do the same.
      *[Bob finds the quickest way out of the forest he can. A little*
      *smile back on the way out. MAUREEN notices the tacklebox.*
      *Thinks for a moment, then…]*
Hey – Wait a minute – you-
      *[MAUREEN is curious. She contemplates the quiet moment.*
      *She opens the tacklebox. There are fishing lures. She breathes*
      *a sigh of relief. Fingering the lures, she pulls out a magazine.*
      *This one she is not so thrilled about. She pulls out a baseball,*

*and finally a baseball card. She takes her bat and clutches it tightly as lights fade.]*

END OF PLAY

# FAMILY 2.0

## WALTER WYKES

*Family 2.0* was originally produced on April 6, 2007, by La Cosa Nostra Productions in Tallahassee, Florida. The production was directed by Seth Federman. The cast was as follows:

WIFE: Rebecca Marchetti
HUSBAND: Kevin Sullivan
SON: Danielle Festa
DAUGHTER: Katerina Gawlak
FIRST HUSBAND/DOG: Jared Hair

SETTING:
A perfect-looking house—the kind you find in magazines.

*[A perfect-looking house—the kind you find in magazines. A perfect-looking WIFE puts the finishing touches on her perfect-looking living room. The front door opens and HUSBAND enters.]*

HUSBAND: Hi, Honey! I'm home!

WIFE: Who are you? What are you doing in my house?!

HUSBAND: I'm your new husband. Where should I put my coat? *[He tries to kiss WIFE, but she backs away from him terrified.]*

WIFE: Don't touch me! I'll scream! I'll call the police!

HUSBAND: Aren't you going to ask how my day was?

WIFE: *[Attempting to pacify him.]* How … how was your day?

HUSBAND: It was awful! Just like every other day! Same old boring job. Same old boring boss. Same old boring life. And then, on the way home, suddenly it hit to me—why come home to the same old boring wife and house and kids and dog when I could try something new?

WIFE: But you can't just—

HUSBAND: I've always admired your home. It's very well kept.

WIFE: Thank you, but—

HUSBAND: I pass it every day on my way to work, so I thought today I'd give it a try. It has to be more exciting than the one I've been coming home to for the past fifteen years.

WIFE: But … I already have a husband.

HUSBAND: He can have my life. Where does he work?

WIFE: He's an executive.  At a technology company.

HUSBAND: Perfect!  I love technology!  All those little gadgets and stuff!  It'll be great!

WIFE: Look, I'm ... I'm sorry your life is so boring.  My life is boring too.  But you can't just walk in here and expect us to—

HUSBAND: Oh!  I almost forgot!  I brought you flowers!
    *[He produces a bouquet of flowers from his coat.]*

WIFE: You brought me flowers?

HUSBAND: They're orchids—a symbol of rare beauty and eternal love—my love for you.

WIFE: My ... my husband hasn't brought me flowers in almost fifteen years.

HUSBAND: I wrote you a poem too.

WIFE: A poem?

HUSBAND: Would you like me to recite it?

WIFE: Well ... if you went to the trouble of writing it ... I ... I wouldn't want it to go to waste.

HUSBAND: You take my breath away.
Like the sunset or a summer day.
When I gaze at the moon
Or the ocean blue
They pale beside the sight of you.
You take my breath away.

WIFE: That's beautiful.  You ... you really wrote that?

HUSBAND: For you.

*[Pause. She considers this.]*

WIFE: Do you pee in the shower?

HUSBAND: Never.

WIFE: Hog the sheets?

HUSBAND: Nope.

WIFE: Snore?

HUSBAND: I don't think so.

WIFE: Any history of baldness in your family?

HUSBAND: On the contrary.  We're very hairy.

WIFE: Would you do your own laundry or wait for me to do it.

HUSBAND: Do it myself.

WIFE: Fix the toilet or call a plumber?

HUSBAND: Fix it.

WIFE: Shingle the roof or buy a new house?

HUSBAND: New house.

WIFE: Anniversary in Maui or Vegas?

HUSBAND: Maui.

WIFE: Watch football or do me in the kitchen?

HUSBAND: Do you really have to ask?

WIFE: Will you constantly try to pork me in the rear?

HUSBAND: Only if you want me to.

WIFE: Tell me about your first wife.

HUSBAND: She was a nag. A nag with no boobs. She had boobs until the baby was born, but he sucked them right off. I'm a boob man, so it was completely unworkable.

WIFE: You left because she lost her boobs?

HUSBAND: There were other things. But I have to be honest—it was mainly the boobs.

WIFE: What if I lose my boobs? Will you leave me too?

HUSBAND: It looks like you've got plenty to spare!
        *[They make out.]*
Can we have sex now?

WIFE: Easy, Tiger. You'll have to win the kids over first. Children!
        *[Enter SON and DAUGHTER.]*
Children, meet your new father.

HUSBAND: Hi, kids.

SON: You're not my father! You're a fake! An imposter!

HUSBAND: Do you like baseball?

SON: Sure.

HUSBAND: I'll take you to the Big Game.

SON: The Big Game?! No way!
        *[He embraces HUSBAND.]*
I love you, Dad!

DAUGHTER: What about me? I hate baseball.

HUSBAND: Do you like shopping?

DAUGHTER: Duh.

HUSBAND: Here—knock yourself out.
    *[He hands her a hundred dollar bill.]*

DAUGHTER: A hundred dollar bill?! You're the greatest!
    *[She kisses HUSBAND on the cheek.]*

WIFE: Go play in your room, kids. Your father and I need some time alone.

DAUGHTER: Sure thing, Mom.

SON: See ya later, Dad.
    *[Exit kids.]*

WIFE: *[Seductively.]* Now where were we?
    *[They make out. Enter FIRST HUSBAND.]*

FIRST HUSBAND: Hi, Honey! I'm ... what's going on here?! What are you doing to my wife?!

HUSBAND: I'm trying to pork her in the rear.

FIRST HUSBAND: I'm calling the police!

WIFE: Wait! Give me your key.

FIRST HUSBAND: What?

WIFE: Your key. Hand it over.

FIRST HUSBAND: I don't understand.

WIFE: He's replacing you.

FIRST HUSBAND: Replacing me?

WIFE: That's right.  He's in—you're out.

FIRST HUSBAND: But why?!

WIFE: He brought me flowers!  When's the last time you brought me flowers?!

FIRST HUSBAND: I—

WIFE: Exactly.  Now stop stuttering and hand over the key.

FIRST HUSBAND: But … what about the kids?!  You can't take the kids away from me!  Kids!
   *[Enter SON and DAUGHTER.]*
You don't want me to go—do you kids?

SON: He's taking me to the Big Game.

FIRST HUSBAND: I'll take you!

SON: Too late.  You had your chance.

FIRST HUSBAND: But—

DAUGHTER: Sorry.  It's nothing personal.

WIFE: *[Her hand outstretched.]*  The key.

FIRST HUSBAND: But I don't want to go!  Please, I'll … I'll do anything!  Just let me stay!  I won't bother you!  I'll stay out of the way!  I'll … I'll be another kid!  Or the family dog!

SON: I've always wanted a dog!

DAUGHTER: Eww! He's gonna get hair everywhere!

SON: Please?! Can I keep him?! Can I?!

WIFE: I don't know. What do you think, Honey?

HUSBAND: He'd be your responsibility, Son. We're not going to feed him for you, or take him for walks, or clean up his poop—

SON: I'll take care of him! I promise!
    *[To FIRST HUSBAND/DOG.]*
Come here, boy! Sit! Roll over! Play dead! Good boy!

FIRST HUSBAND/DOG: Woof! Woof!

DAUGHTER: Can I go shopping now?

WIFE: If your father will drive you.

DAUGHTER: Dad?

HUSBAND: Well … your mother and I were sort of in the middle of something.

DAUGHTER: But I want to go now! There's a sale!

FIRST HUSBAND/DOG: Woof! Woof!

HUSBAND: Okay, just give us—

FIRST HUSBAND/DOG: Woof!

WIFE: I think the dog has to go.

HUSBAND: Son, take your dog outside.

SON: I can't. I have homework.
    *[Exit SON.]*

DAUGHTER: Can I go shopping or not?

FIRST HUSBAND/DOG: Woof!  Woof!

WIFE: Honey, could you take care of the dog?

HUSBAND: It's not my dog.

WIFE: You told him he could keep it.

FIRST HUSBAND/DOG: Woof!

HUSBAND: Do we have a leash?

DAUGHTER: Is anybody listening to me?
        *[Enter SON with baseball and glove.]*

SON: Hey Dad, can we play ball?

HUSBAND: I thought you had homework.

SON: I just finished.

DAUGHTER: Hello?

FIRST HUSBAND/DOG: Woof!  Woof!

HUSBAND: *[To SON.]*  Here—take the dog outside.

SON: I have to poop.
        *[Exit SON.]*

WIFE: *[To HUSBAND]*  While you're out, can you take the trash?

FIRST HUSBAND/DOG: Woof!

HUSBAND: Ahh … sure.

DAUGHTER: I hate this family!

WIFE: And could you do something about your daughter?

FIRST HUSBAND/DOG: Woof!

HUSBAND: What do you want me to—

FIRST HUSBAND/DOG: Woof! Woof!

HUSBAND: *[To FIRST HUSBAND/DOG]* Shut up, you stupid mutt!

FIRST HUSBAND/DOG: Grrr!
*[FIRST HUSBAND/DOG bites HUSBAND'S pants and pulls him towards the door.]*

WIFE: I think he really wants to go.

DAUGHTER: What about me?! Does anybody care what I want?!
*[Enter SON.]*

SON: The Big Game starts any minute! We have to go!

HUSBAND: *[To WIFE]* When … when we get back it would be really nice to have some quality alone time if you know what I mean.

WIFE: It'll have to wait, Dear. You have responsibilities now.

HUSBAND: Responsibilities?! This isn't what I signed up for! You're just like my first wife!

WIFE: WHAT did you say?!!!

HUSBAND: I—

WIFE: Don't compare me to that flat-chested bitch!

HUSBAND: I didn't mean—

WIFE: Do you see these tits?!  Do you ever want to touch these tits again?!

HUSBAND: Yes!  Yes, I do!  That's what I—

FIRST HUSBAND/DOG: Woof!  Woof!

SON: We're gonna miss the game!  We have to go NOW!

DAUGHTER: I asked first!  It's not fair!

WIFE: If I ever hear you even THINK her name again—

DAUGHTER: You can't just ignore me!

SON: You promised!

WIFE: I swear to God—

FIRST HUSBAND/DOG: Woof!
> *[As the cacophony rises, everyone converges on HUSBAND who climbs onto the couch to escape them.  They surround him like a pack of rabid wolves.]*

| WIFE | SON | DAUGHTER | DOG |
|---|---|---|---|
| Your balls will | All I wanted to | Am I invisible? | Woof! |
| be so blue you'll | do was go to | Am I not even | Woof! |
| be begging me | the Big Game! | here?  What do I | Woof! |
| to fuck *you* in | But now it's | have to do to get | Woof! |
| the ass!  Are you | too late!  I | some attention in | Woof! |
| hearing me?! | already told all | this house?!  Do | Woof! |
| Are we clear on | of my friends | I have to shoot | Woof! |
| this?!  It's gonna | we were | somebody?  Do I | Woof! |
| take a LOT of | going, and | have to blow | Woof! |
| ass-kissing to | they're all | something up? | Woof! |
| make up for this | going too, and | Maybe I should | Woof! |
| little slip-up, | now they're | get pregnant!  I | Woof! |
| Mister!  Not | going to see | should find the | Woof! |

only am I not *like* her, but she doesn't exist! She's a figment of your imagination! She's not even a figment! I am the first and *only* woman you've ever loved, buddy, and you will grovel at my feet if you want any pudding from my kitchen!

that I'm not really there and they're going to know what losers we are! I'll bet you didn't even buy tickets—did you?! Liar! My other Dad would have taken me! I should have gone with him! I'm never going to believe another word you say! You're a big fat ugly liar!

first boy who wants to fuck me and just pull up my skirt! There are plenty of boys at school who'd like to fuck me! Maybe they already have! Maybe I just haven't told you! Or maybe I have but you don't fucking listen!

Woof!
Woof!
Woof!
Woof!
Woof!
Woof!
Woof!
Woof!
Woof!
Woof!
Woof!
Woof!
Woof!
Woof!
Woof!
Woof!
Woof!
Woof!
Woof!
Woof!
Woof!
Woof!
Woof!

HUSBAND: I NEED A NEW LIFE!!!
    *[Blackout.]*

\* \* \*

# THE NEXT MRS. JACOB ANDERSON

## ANN WUEHLER

*The Next Mrs. Jacob Anderson* was originally produced at the American High School at Bitburg Air Force Base in Bitburg, Germany. The production was directed by Jade Thrasher. The cast was as follows:

MRS. JACOB ANDERSON: Ahkira Rogers
LISA: Kimberly Strong

SETTING:
A Farmer's Market. A stand of vegetables and fruits. Very picked over. Prices per dozen, per pound, etc, stuck here and there. Afternoon. The here and now.

*[As the lights come up, we see LISA, a youngish woman wearing jeans. She is smiling, delighted with life. She examines tomatoes and cucumbers, stopping to stare dreamily off into space. MRS. JACOB ANDERSEN comes into the playing area, carrying a plastic sack of produce. She is a little older than Lisa. Both women are ordinary-looking, with ordinary bodies.]*

MRS. ANDERSEN: My...there's not much left here today.

LISA: Oh I know.
*[A frown flits across her face. She studies Mrs. Andersen from the corner of her eye. Mrs. Andersen notices but does not seem to mind.]*

MRS. ANDERSEN: They usually have such gorgeous cukes here.

LISA: I guess you have to get here early.

MRS. ANDERSEN: I think you're right.
*[Silence. Mrs. Andersen comes down front as if looking at the sky, at the surrounding countryside.]*
I know you're fucking my husband.
*[Lisa goes very still, like a threatened spider. She does not know what to do. Mrs. Andersen continues to serenely gaze at the 'sky'.]*
Isn't it a beautiful day? Not many left.

LISA: I...I think you have me confused with...

MRS. ANDERSEN: No. I don't.

LISA: Well this has been...

MRS. ANDERSEN: Yes. Awkward. Stereotypical...many things. He wants to divorce me and make you Mrs. Andersen. A woman without her own name.

LISA: You're...Jacob's wife.

53

MRS. ANDERSEN: Yes. And that right there should make you run screaming. *[Looks over her shoulder at Lisa.]* At first I wanted to kill you. Not him. You. I imagined running you through all sorts of industrial machines.

LISA: He loves me. I'm sorry this hurts you...

MRS. ANDERSEN: Love is an anesthesia. It puts you to sleep, it allows you to overlook, not question, not care...and then, one day, you come to. And, by God and all his horny angels...it's an eye opener.

LISA: Look. I didn't mean for any of this to happen. I'm not a bad person...I didn't want to fall in love but I did. And we're happy. Is that what this is about? He said you'd...

MRS. ANDERSEN: Are you the next Mrs. Jacob Andersen?
*[Lisa comes forward, determined to have this out.]*

LISA: Can't we be adult about this?

MRS. ANDERSEN: No. Adults are never honest. Let's be children. Let's throw rocks, let's weep and say everything we actually think. But we won't.

LISA: Okay, look. He hasn't loved you for a long time. Don't you have any pride?

MRS. ANDERSEN: Tons of it. An ocean of it. Why don't you? Why do you love him? He says you can't find a job right now. He says you're so pretty and so nice. Nice—you're what every man wants a woman to be. Nice.
*[Mrs. Andersen smiles very gently at Lisa, beckons her closer. Lisa does not move.]*
Here we are...both picking out vegetables for the same man.

LISA: He's right. You are a bitch.

MRS. ANDERSEN: Yes, I suppose so. A bitch, a cunt, a twat...why is it always bitch that stings? Oh yes, that's right—it implies I'm not as nice as I should be. That I've revealed too much of myself. Well ... Lisa, is it? What a cheerleader sort of name. Do you cheerlead for him now? Tell him he's the best, the brightest, the bravest? I can see you doing it. With pompoms in your hands. With that little flippy skirt. You'd look nice in navy. *[Sighs. But still steady and calm.]* I once had a name. But now it's bitch and second-best. It's Mrs. Andersen. Why would you give up your name? Why would you let him erase it from your head with his acid? His sweet...numbing acid...I'll take care of you, I'll take care of everything.

LISA: Wow. That's some speech. Save it for group therapy sometime...
        *[Mrs. Andersen catches Lisa by the arm.]*
Hey. Don't.

MRS. ANDERSEN: Please. Tell me why you love him. Tell me everything...and we never have to talk again. I'll step aside. I'll...let you have him. I'll disappear. I'll be like an abortion in your lives...something that never happened, something that was scraped into a pail. *[Looks into Lisa's face, releases her, steps away.]* Surely...if you love him you won't mind facing your enemy. We can go somewhere else if you wish.

LISA: No. Harriman's Market is just fine. I...I just tell you whatever and you go away? Just like a big puff of smoke?

MRS. ANDERSEN: You betcha.

LISA: You betcha.
        *[Silence. The two contemplate each other.]*
Jacob says you lie.

MRS. ANDERSEN: That's...very funny.

LISA: I think it's sad. It's probably why you two just didn't work out. I feel sorry for you.

MRS. ANDERSEN: That's funny, too. Because I feel sorry for you. Here we are with pity in our hearts...all this pity and no place to put it away for good.
   *[Pause.]*
Do you pity me when you're beneath him?

LISA: Don't be disgusting. He said you could be disgusting.

MRS. ANDERSEN: It's just us. Are you going to tell him of this meeting? I'm not.

LISA: Of course I'm going to tell him. I don't keep secrets.

MRS. ANDERSEN: Fucking a married man in your car is a secret. Giving him blow jobs parked on the side of the freeway is a secret...He tells me things, too, my dear.
   *[Lisa sniffs, turns away for a moment.]*
And how alive he feels, how refreshed. You're just like a glass of iced tea.

LISA: Ummm. I think I've had enough of this...

MRS. ANDERSEN: Lisa. All I want is a confession. Is that so hard? Can you face me and confess...confess how you love my husband?
   *[Lisa puts her hand into the vegetables. She examines them.]*
It's hard, isn't it. Sleeping with him is easy. Telling me about it...difficult. Yet...you say you have no secrets.

LISA: Not from Jacob! I don't have secrets from the man I love, the man I'm going to spend the rest of my life with. Got that? You want a confession? Here it is. We met, we fought against it, we gave in because it's right, it feels right. And yeah...I fuck him. I fuck him with nothing held back.
   *[Silence.]*
So get on your broomstick and take a left turn.

MRS. ANDERSEN: The second Mrs. Jacob Andersen.
   *[Lisa stops from leaving.]*

LISA: The only Mrs. Andersen.

MRS. ANDERSEN: No. There are many nameless women behind you...many before you. You are not the only one. And what a beautiful love story. We met, we fought it, we fucked. Spare, succinct, to the point. Nothing flowery or pretty. Just bodies and selfishness.

LISA: How dare you...how dare you...

MRS. ANDERSEN: Because I looked in the mirror one day. I looked and I could not see myself. I had no face, no features. There was only...Mrs. Jacob Andersen...a wife, a woman with no children, a woman who helps out in her church.

LISA: Well maybe you should get out more.

MRS. ANDERSEN: Shh...listen. You see...I had a sort of vision. A presentiment...a feeling of doom. Not for me...for you. For all women like you.

LISA: Women like me...?!

MRS. ANDERSEN: Women who give up their identities....their souls...the secret sweetness of their hearts. I saw in my mirror many women...of all sizes, all shapes. With kinky hair, with straight, with curly and short. With wide dark faces, narrow pale ones, and every sort of face in between...

LISA: You're crazy...he never said you were crazy...
        [Mrs. Andersen takes Lisa by the wrist.]
Let me go.

MRS. ANDERSEN: All these different, glorious women. And then came this mist, this fog. It covered them, every one. And it took their faces and made them all the same. And I was so afraid...so afraid. Because they were dead. They had given up their faces, their names...and now they were dead in that mist. And they were lost. As I was lost since I was fourteen.

LISA: I'm...I'm not faceless. You're...just trying to get him back.

MRS. ANDERSEN: No. I want someone much more important back.

LISA: His money?

MRS. ANDERSEN: Don't be obtuse.

LISA: He's a great guy! He said you'd act all crazy and spooky...

MRS. ANDERSEN: What are you, twelve? Are you some twelve year old who believes everything a boy tells her? Everything? If you love me you'll do as I ask, as I demand with no giving back, with no giving back??!!
        *[Silence. Lisa stares determinedly away. Mrs. Andersen steps back toward the vegetables, fingers them.]*
Some day, it's going to be you here in my place, a name with nothing to it, looking at a young, stupid woman. Because it won't end with you. Jacob always tires of his new toys.

LISA: No. He tired of you! He got tired of your whiny, bitchy ways. That's what he said. He said you fooled him, that you weren't honest...

MRS. ANDERSEN: Of course I wasn't. What women is honest, ever, with a man? Can you imagine the horror if we told them what we really feel, what we really think?

LISA: He said...

MRS. ANDERSEN: He said, he said!! What about you? What do you say?
        *[Lisa frowns. Mrs. Andersen approaches her.]*
You say nothing, is that it? His voice, never your voice. What he wants, what he needs. Always. I know. I know all about it...

LISA: What you know, lady, is that you've lost. You fucked up by not loving him enough. Jacob says he froze being in the same room with you.

MRS. ANDERSEN: Of course he did. I grew warm and he grew cold.

LISA: We're done talking or whatever this is.

MRS. ANDERSEN: Lisa. A confession. Admit what you did. Not what he did. What you did.

LISA: I told you already.

MRS. ANDERSEN: No. You mouthed what he wants you to say!!

LISA: He said you'd be like this. That you wouldn't understand.
   *[Silence. Mrs. Andersen starts laughing. Lisa ducks her head defensively.]*

MRS. ANDERSEN: Do you know he cheated on his girlfriend with me? And he told me how understanding and nice I was, so much more understanding than her, the other twat in his life. That's what he called her—the other twat. No name, just known by her one body part, which he had grown tired of. I was so flattered. Like you are. So glad that such a handsome man would ever look my way. So full of this grinning glad power that I had stolen him from a much prettier girl. Not allowing myself to know that I had not stolen him at all—that he just needed a new hole.
   *[Pause.]*
Women don't talk like this. Do we. We talk about feelings and love and the heart. We don't mention dicks or assholes or pussies. It's disgusting and disturbing for women to say such things—for good girls to say such things.

LISA: You were his first girlfriend and first wife...

MRS. ANDERSEN: No. You're not listening. I wish you to be free. I wish you to keep your cheerleader name. Because you won't last. He'll burn through you like a grass fire. You'll be ashes and tears by the time he's moved on.

LISA: He's not moving on. He is not ever moving on. You're so disgusting!

MRS. ANDERSEN: I am, I quite agree. You're already cracked about the edges, a dish with chipped edges. I can see it. He did that to you. Oh he didn't mean to, he probably really does love you or whatever he bothers to feel.
   *[Pause.]*
I just wanted to warn you.

LISA: No...you wanted to be a total bitch. You wanted revenge because I make him happy and you don't...

MRS. ANDERSEN: Oh dear, were you speaking? You don't seem to have any lips. Or a face, for that matter. I feel so sorry for you. I really do. I hated you until someone pointed out who you were. And...since you're not leaving, some part of you knows...

LISA: I love him. He loves me. We are gonna have everything you never had...including children.

MRS. ANDERSEN: You're pregnant?

LISA: Not yet.

MRS. ANDERSEN: Congratulations when you are. He likes his steaks fried with onions, there's some nice ones here still. You know, my dear Lisa...there've been others...besides you. And he promised them, too, he would leave me and marry them. How stupid...how stupid are you?
   *[Their eyes meet and lock. Lisa tosses her head.]*

LISA: How stupid are you to stay?

MRS. ANDERSEN: I'm not. When he comes home from work tonight...he'll find his clothes in suitcases, his possessions neatly boxed up. I was going to burn everything, including the house. How expected. Goodbye, my dear. Goodbye, Mrs. Andersen, part two.

LISA: *[Whispers this.]*  He's a wonderful man.
    *[Mrs. Andersen exits as Lisa stares after her. Blackout.]*


END of PLAY

# THE CHOCOLATE AFFAIR

STEPHANIE ALISON WALKER

*The Chocolate Affair* was first produced at Glendale Community College in Glendale, CA, as part of the Motel Chronicles Series on June 6, 2008, directed by Kim Turnbull, with the following cast:

BEVERLY: Mary Claire Garcia
MR. GOODBAR: Chris Beltran
M&M: Nancy Yalley

SETTING:
A seedy motel room.

*[Lights up on BEVERLY (33)—well put together, slim and wearing flattering and feminine business attire. She cradles a plastic Halloween pumpkin filled with candy.]*

*[She looks around the room and carefully sets the pumpkin on the bed. She looks at it for a beat, then closes the blinds, shutting out any hint of the outside.]*

*[She sits on the bed next to the pumpkin.]*

BEVERLY: This is crazy.
*[She looks at the pumpkin. Then away. Then at the pumpkin. And away. At the pumpkin. Away. Then she practically lunges at it, reaches in and pulls out a piece of candy.]*

*[She holds the candy before her. She sniffs it, deeply inhaling its scent. She unwraps it and carefully takes a bite. Slowly. Savoring every morsel. She moans. This is ecstasy.]*

*[She digs back into the pumpkin and excitedly dumps all the contents onto the bed. She rolls around in the candy. Laughing. Devouring piece after piece after piece.]*

*[She begins to choke. And then recovers. She's silent for a few moments. Long enough for sadness to set in.]*

*[MR. GOODBAR appears and sits next to her on the bed. He puts his arm around her.]*

MR. GOODBAR: Don't be sad, Bev.

BEVERLY: Holy crap!

MR. GOODBAR: Whoa, whoa, whoa. It's okay.

BEVERLY: Who are you? What are you doing here?!

MR. GOODBAR: You brought me here.

BEVERLY: I...

MR. GOODBAR: You brought all of us here.
        *[He gestures to the candy on the bed.]*

BEVERLY: You're...

MR. GOODBAR: Mr. Goodbar.

BEVERLY: I've had way too much sugar.

MR. GOODBAR: Are you okay, Bev?

BEVERLY: I shouldn't be here.

MR. GOODBAR: You wanted to be alone with us.

BEVERLY: Yes.

MR. GOODBAR: Have another piece of candy.

BEVERLY: I shouldn't.

MR. GOODBAR: If you can't eat candy when you're alone in a seedy
motel room, when can you?
        *[He hands her a piece of candy. She eats it. It makes her
        happy.]*

MR. GOODBAR: That worked, didn't it?

BEVERLY: Yeah.
        *[He sits on the bed with legs outstretched and leans against
        the headboard.]*

BEVERLY: I love chocolate and peanuts.

MR. GOODBAR: That's me. Mr. Goodbar. Chocolate and peanuts.

BEVERLY: I love you.

MR. GOODBAR: C'mere.
   *[She lays back against him holding the pumpkin on her stomach.]*

MR. GOODBAR: Have another.
   *[She reaches and grabs a mini bag of M&Ms. She rips it open and pulls out an M&M.]*

M&M: Stop!

BEVERLY: Who said that?
   *[An M&M enters in person form.]*

M&M: What the heck do you think you're doing?

BEVERLY: I'm...I'm....nothing. Nothing.

MR. GOODBAR: For your information, she is giving herself a break.

BEVERLY: Yeah.

MR. GOODBAR: A well-deserved break.

BEVERLY: Well-deserved.

MR. GOODBAR: Hard earned.

BEVERLY: I work so hard.

MR. GOODBAR: And she never gets to eat candy.

BEVERLY: Never. I never do.

M&M: But this isn't your candy to eat.

BEVERLY: Yes it is.

M&M: No it's not. It's Sally's candy.

MR. GOODBAR: Sally?

M&M: Sally. You know. Ten years old. Pig tails. Pirate.

MR. GOODBAR: Oh, the pirate girl. *(to BEV)* Is this true?

BEVERLY: No.

MR. GOODBAR: Bev?

BEVERLY: It's not true.

M&M: It is true. Your daughter Sally earned this candy. She trick or treated for this candy.

MR. GOODBAR: You stole this candy from your daughter?

BEVERLY: I didn't steal it.

MR. GOODBAR: And she made such a cute little pirate.

BEVERLY: She's a pirate every year.
  *[She reaches for another piece of candy and M&M fights her for it. They fight over the candy.]*

M&M: It's not yours!

BEVERLY: Give it!

M&M: I won't let you eat your daughter's candy!

BEVERLY: But I'm helping her!
  *[BEV rips the candy away from M&M and eats it.]*

MR. GOODBAR: You're helping her?

BEVERLY: Yes.

MR. GOODBAR: *(to M&M)* See? She's helping her.

M&M: How is she helping her?

MR. GOODBAR: *(to Bev)* How are you helping her?

BEVERLY: Sally's not allowed to eat candy.

M&M: Oh please.

BEVERLY: It's true!

M&M: That's pathetic.

BEVERLY: The kids at school... they make fun of her. They call her Miss Piggy.

MR. GOODBAR: Oh, that's awful. Kids are so mean!

BEVERLY: She comes home in tears some days and won't tell me why. But I know why.

M&M: Because she's fat?

BEVERLY: *(softly)* Yes.

M&M: So she's a chubster, huh?

MR. GOODBAR: M&M, have some tact.

BEVERLY: She can't help it. She just loves candy so much. And tater tots. And pizza and chips. The other kids eat the same things and they don't get fat. How is that fair? It's not. Not one bit. The other day, I caught her melting cheese on a plate. To eat. As a snack. Just cheese melted on a plate.

M&M: That's disgusting.

BEVERLY: And of all the candy in the world, M&M, you're her favorite. She loves you the most.

MR. GOODBAR: That's sweet. I'm not jealous.

M&M: So Sally's a little chubby McChubster. A piggly wiggly.

MR. GOODBAR: Stop!

M&M: A rolly polly pirate girl?

MR. GOODBAR: Wait a second. The pirate girl was skinny.

M&M: Right. She was a beanpole. The only pig feature about her were her tails.

MR. GOODBAR: So Sally's not fat?

M&M: Sally—Bev's daughter, the pirate girl, the rightful owner of this here candy—is not fat.

MR. GOODBAR: Bev? Is this true?
     *[BEV ignores the question and eats another piece of candy.]*

MR. GOODBAR: It's all a lie?

M&M: You bet it's a lie.

MR. GOODBAR: I don't understand. What kind of person...

M&M: Come on Goodbar, let's get out of here.

MR. GOODBAR: Beverly... why?

M&M: Don't talk to her. She's pathetic! Help me with the candy.
     *[M&M starts gathering it up. MR. GOODBAR doesn't move.]*

M&M: Come on, Goodbar! Help me.

MR. GOODBAR: Bev?!

M&M: Grab the candy.

MR. GOODBAR: Talk to us, Bev!

M&M: Save your breath. She's just gonna lie.

BEVERLY: I can't take it anymore!!
    *[M&M stops. A long beat. They watch Bev.]*

BEVERLY: I'm up every day at five. Every day. Up at five, go for a
jog, take a shower, wake Sally, cook breakfast—something healthy-
egg whites, flax, kale, organic coffee, sprouted wheat. Sit down with
Dave and Sally for breakfast. Eat a tiny portion. Be sure to leave some
on the plate. Always leave some on the plate.

Get dressed. Something feminine, flattering. Kiss Dave goodbye.
Make sure to give him a little something worth coming back home to.

Check on Sally. Comb her hair. Pack her lunch. Wait with her for the
bus. Hug her goodbye. Make sure that hug lasts all day long...that she
feels your arms around her even at recess when the mean kids pick on
her because their moms don't hug them enough. Then let go. Watch
her walk away, board the bus.

Choke back your tears. Taste the salt slide down the back of your
throat. Go back inside. Check yourself in the mirror. Ugh. Turn
around. Turn back hoping to see someone else. Cross through the
kitchen. Pause. Feel the quiet of the empty house. No one watching.
What can you eat? Open the pantry, look inside. Grab the jar of
peanut butter. Unscrew the lid. Take a whiff. Stick your finger in the
jar of peanut butter. Lick it off. Feel someone watching you. Shit.
Turn around to face them. No one's there. Put the peanut butter away.
Wash your hands, careful to remove any trace of peanut butter.
Reapply lipstick. Head out the door. To work. Again.

*[A long pause.]*

M&M: *(a revelation)* You used to be fat.

MR. GOODBAR: M&M!

M&M: Oh, please. I know her type. *(to BEVERLY)* How much?

BEVERLY: My stomach hurts.

M&M: A hundred? Huh? How much?

MR. GOODBAR: A hundred what?

M&M: Pounds. *(to BEV)* Come on. How much did you lose?

BEVERLY: This isn't fun anymore.

M&M: She stole hard earned Halloween candy from her daughter, ditched work and checked herself into a seedy motel to eat it.

BEVERLY: There's something wrong with me.

MR. GOODBAR: She can't help it.

BEVERLY: I'm a terrible person.

M&M: I'd bet at least 110. Am I right? You lost 110 pounds?

MR. GOODBAR: Why 110?

M&M: She's got at least another whole person in here. *(she points at her head)* And she walks like she used to waddle.
  *[BEVERLY throws a piece of candy at M&M and hits her in the head.]*

M&M: Ouch!

MR. GOODBAR: That wasn't nice.

BEVERLY: You're supposed to make me feel better.

MR. GOODBAR: It's okay. Here. Have a Kit Kat.

BEVERLY: I don't want a Kit Kat.

MR. GOODBAR: Sure you do. It always makes you feel better.
*[She takes the Kit Kat and unwraps it. She takes a bite and disappears into her happy place.]*

M&M: No amount of candy will be enough to bury it for good. To make you forget about the chubby little girl nobody loves who melts cheese on a plate and sneaks french fries when nobody's looking and eats M&Ms like we were candy coated pieces of happiness.

MR. GOODBAR: You are candy coated pieces of happiness.

M&M: Thank you. I mean, we try.
*[She finishes the Kit Kat. Swallows slowly and reaches for another piece.]*

M&M: You better not.

MR. GOODBAR: Yeah, you probably shouldn't.

BEVERLY: Why?

M&M: Uh, cuz you'll get fat.

BEVERLY: I'm already fat.

MR. GOODBAR: No.

BEVERLY: Yes.

M&M: She's fat on the inside.

MR. GOODBAR: M&M!

M&M: *(to BEV)* Maybe you should... *(looking at the bathroom)* ...you know. *(sticking finger down throat.)*

BEVERLY: I don't do that!

MR. GOODBAR: Then what are you gonna do?

M&M: What are you gonna tell Sally?

MR. GOODBAR: She'll probably be missing her candy.

M&M: And Dave.

MR. GOODBAR: You'll just have to go back and pretend like this never happened.

M&M: Buy more candy for Sally.

MR. GOODBAR: Fill up the pumpkin. Put it back in her room. Cook a healthy dinner.

M&M: Vegan butternut squash soup and Baby Arugula salad.

MR. GOODBAR: With pine nuts.

M&M: With pine nuts.

MR. GOODBAR: Just pretend this never happened. You can do that. You're good at pretending.

M&M: Lying.

BEVERLY: I stole candy from my own daughter.

MR. GOODBAR: It's okay.

BEVERLY: She could eat this whole pumpkin and not gain a pound.

M&M: Poor Sally.

BEVERLY: I won't do it again.

MR. GOODBAR: I know.

BEVERLY: Vegan butternut squash soup.

MR. GOODBAR: And Baby Arugula salad.

BEVERLY: With pine nuts.

MR. GOODBAR: A healthy supper.

BEVERLY: We'll sit down at the table.

MR. GOODBAR: Like any other day.

BEVERLY: And say grace.

MR. GOODBAR: And it will all be okay.

BEVERLY: Okay.

M&M: And if not...

MR. GOODBAR: We're always here for you.
    *[A long beat.]*

BEVERLY: *(I wish I didn't need you)* I know.
    *[Lights fade to black as BEVERLY slowly puts herself back
    together.]*


END OF PLAY

# NO SUCH THING

DOUGLAS HILL

*No Such Thing* was developed at the University of Nevada, Las Vegas under the direction of Michael Tylo. The cast was as follows:

STEVEN: Doug Milliron
ALAN: Julian C. Smit

SETTING:
The lobby of a Las Vegas Hotel Convention Center, 2006.

*[STEVEN and ALAN sit in typical hotel convention center furniture, huddled over the corner of a small coffee table. Their laptop cases or briefcases lean casually against the furniture. Both men are dressed in slacks, jackets, and ties.]*

ALAN: Honestly? I thought it was great.

STEVEN: Yeah?

ALAN: I thought it was probably one of the best things you've ever written. I'm so proud of you. *Thank you* for sending it to me.

STEVEN: *[letting his grin overtake him]* That's—That's great. I'm glad you liked it.

ALAN: Confidentially: you may have just saved my job for me.

STEVEN: Nnahh. I was glad to do it. Did your boss say—What did your boss think?
    *[Beat.]*

ALAN: Bob…well. Bob liked it, too. Except. The pseudonym. The pseudonym is a problem for us.

STEVEN: It is?

ALAN: That's our policy. You didn't know that, I take it.

STEVEN: No. It's not—when you asked me to submit, you didn't mention—

ALAN: Yeah, we don't do anonymous either.

STEVEN: So…he's—what? He's not going to print it?

ALAN: Oh, no. He loved it, yeah. He's gung ho to publish it in the next issue. But the pseudonym.
    *[Beat. ALAN fixes STEVEN with an expectant stare.]*

79

STEVEN: You told him it was a pseudonym?
*[Pause.]*

ALAN: He would've found out about it sooner or later. And it's your style. I mean, it couldn't get any more apparent that it's your style of writing. But this is cleaner, you know? It's almost a distillation of your style. Like I said, this is some of the best stuff you've ever written. I couldn't wait to show it to Bob.

STEVEN: Did you...Did you...?

ALAN: Um—yeah. That's why I wanted to find you before the conference ended tomorrow, and you left to go back—

STEVEN: *[becoming nervous]* Oh, God—is he going to—

ALAN: Let me tell you how we can make this work.

STEVEN: I can't come out on this piece, Alan. I can't. I live in—it's Utah. We've got a new Dean at the college, and he's very nice and very supportive and very *Mormon.*

ALAN: —I know—

STEVEN: And that would be the end of the job for me. They'd fire me in a heartbeat. I can't come out on this piece.

ALAN: *[nodding]* The Catholics are in the same boat. We're all being drug back into the dark ages. But in all honesty, Bob has a very small subscription base outside of California. And frankly, we need your piece. This is far and above what we normally get from our—

STEVEN: But he can't run that essay without my pseudonym. It'll *kill* me. You've got to tell him that. It would take away everything.

ALAN: Let me tell you what—

STEVEN: There's no negotiating here! I'm dead serious!

ALAN: Steven. I showed Bob those other things you wrote on the internet. Under the pseudonym. And he loved those, too. He's really impressed with you. He said you could freelance for the rest of your life with absolutely no problem.

STEVEN: I don't want to freelance; I want to teach.

ALAN: I know. And let me tellya, Bob was surprised to find out you teach PoliSci in Utah, because you *write* like someone from—

STEVEN: You told him where I work?

ALAN: Not the exact college.

STEVEN: How much did you out me?

ALAN: Bob said he'd pitch you for other jobs with some of his friends around L.A. That's how much he was impressed. This could lead to something big for you. For all of us. He's asking *me* how many other friends I have hidden away who can write like you.

STEVEN: I know this is supposed to be a compliment...But if I lose my job because he prints my real name—I can't afford to live in L.A. on freelance work. I've got great benefits in Utah. I like my teaching job!

ALAN: Look, it's a good essay. It's a *great* essay. You make a million points in it that are smart—God are they smart. Every gay man in the country should be reading this piece. Do you realize how easily you could become a leading national figure for us?

STEVEN: But then all it takes is one Google search or Lexis-Nexis and I'm out of work. *(Exhale.)* Forget it, Alan. I'll...I don't know. I'm sorry—I'll submit it somewhere else.

ALAN: Well, Steven...I mean, Jesus. Are you really going to jerk me around like this? You send me your stuff, and I get *my* boss all excited about it, and now you just decide to take it back?

STEVEN: I'm sorry, but—

ALAN: I mean this isn't about your job alone. We're talking about my job too, here.

STEVEN: Tell Bob I got cold feet. Tell him—

ALAN: Why did you even bother? I mean, this is obviously not about "publish or perish." If you wanted to *just* be a teacher, why did you write this piece in the first place? Or anything else for that matter?

STEVEN: Because you asked me to. And I believe in what I wrote. I think it's a good essay.

ALAN: So do I. Don't get me wrong. But you don't think anyone else should know that you wrote it?

STEVEN: It doesn't matter that people know it's me. What matters is the thought.

ALAN: To be perfectly honest, Steven, I think what matters is that you're willing to let these Mormon jerks terrorize you into a corner.

STEVEN: Alan, Dean Burton is not a jerk. He's been very supportive of me and even got me a per diem for my meals here at the conference this year. The last thing that—

ALAN: Because he thought you were straight, buddy. You got a heterosexual per diem. Not a gay one.

STEVEN: They don't make gay per diems.

ALAN: Not in Utah, they don't.

STEVEN: And they don't make heterosexual ones—

ALAN: Don't even kid yourself. Don't *even* kid yourself.

STEVEN: Burton is a good man.  And he supports—

ALAN: Who thinks you're straight.

STEVEN: He supports me—do you know how hard it was for me to get to this conference last year?  Do you—do you know how hard I had to fight to get administrative leave from my classes?  Burton came on in July and practically handed me the—the travel docs, the per diem—

ALAN: Because he thought you were straight.  And this, if I'm not mistaken, is the one of the points in your essay.  But in real life, you let him push you into the closet rather than—

STEVEN: Okay, maybe you're right!  And if I worked at UCLA or UNLV or U. of A., I could get a—a *gay* per diem.  But I work in the heart of the Mormon Territory—

ALAN: —Good ole Hetero Happy Valley—

STEVEN: —And guess what: I work with people I like.  This is a good job for me.  And the minute Burton finds out I'm gay, I'll get the axe.  Alan, I've got a mortgage.

ALAN: Thank God the man is so supportive.

STEVEN: Okay, this is *your* cause.  It's—it's not mine.  I don't wrap myself in the rainbow and do the parade.  You know that.  You've always known—

ALAN: No, you'd rather pretend to be something you're not so you can get a per diem…A fucking per diem, Steven!  Think about it.  It's like prostituting yourself for dinner.  Wouldn't you rather set an example?  I'm sure there must be some little gay Mormon boy in your class needing a role model.  Am I right?

STEVEN: Not everyone is *you*, Alan.  Some gay men prefer to be a little more discreet.

ALAN: —give me a break—

STEVEN: My students and co-workers don't have to know everything about me; and here's a little news flash: Having a private life works out just fine for me.

ALAN: You're not acting like a private person when you write essays like the one you just sent me. Don't you think it's time you finally had the courage of your convictions?
    *[Pause.]*

STEVEN: Goodbye. Maybe I'll see you here next year.

ALAN: Come on, Steven. Stop running away from this. If you asked everybody at this conference what they thought about a smart, articulate, gay political science teacher—

STEVEN: —Would you keep your voice down?—

ALAN: —who in this day and age—under this presidential administration!—chooses of his own free will to stay hidden in the closet; most of them would say there's no such thing. But this is what you're doing because someone at a Mormon college is promising you a free lunch.

STEVEN: Well maybe you shouldn't have asked me to write something in the first place. You know? Maybe you should have begged an essay from some other ex-boyfriend; some other over-the-top drag queen who needs to be the center of attention at your fabulous L.A. gay soirees. I'll just take my essay and submit it to a magazine that doesn't have your self-righteous mission to out every gay man in America.

ALAN: Well, you can't.
    *[Beat.]*

STEVEN: I'll submit it wherever I want.

ALAN: *We're* running the essay. It's going to print on Monday.
   *[Pause.]*
That's why I wanted to talk with you before the conference ended.

STEVEN: I didn't—You can't print it without a contract. I haven't signed anything. I'll sue you so fast, your goddamn head will spin off.

ALAN: We're not running it as a feature. It's in our op/ed section.

STEVEN: ...what?

ALAN: All submissions to our op/ed department immediately become property of the magazine.

STEVEN: You sonofabitch, I sent it to you as a feature.

ALAN: I'm not the features editor, you know that.

STEVEN: But you're supposed to be my friend.

ALAN: And I got Bob to cut you a check for the essay. We don't normally pay for the op/ed.

STEVEN: Alan, please—I am begging you: Tell Bob this was all a big mistake. Tell him that it's not an op/ed—

ALAN: It's too good an essay for us not to run it. I personally know men who have been waiting for an essay like this. This is going to make a difference.
   *[Beat. STEVEN is crushed, lost, adrift.]*
And you're not the only one with a mortgage, Steven.

STEVEN: You asked me to send you—you said you were. . . Why are you doing this to me?

ALAN: Jesus, buddy. In the big picture, this has very little to do with you.

*[STEVEN throws a right punch and knocks ALAN to the floor. STEVEN towers over him.]*

BLACKOUT

# HEART OF HEARING

JOSEPH ZECCOLA

*Heart of Hearing* premiered at the University of Nevada, Las Vegas on March 8, 1995, under the direction of Michael Serna. The cast was as follows:

ANGIE: Christy Zollar
JOSH: Christopher Keefe

SETTING:
Angie's room. Josh's room.

Copyright © 1995 by Joseph Zeccola

*[ANGIE sits on her bed, the phone is at her ear.]*

ANGIE: *[Practicing to herself.]* Hey, what's up? ... What's up? ... How's it going? ... Sorry I blew you off last year, but how the hell are ya? ... That's good.
> *[Pause.]*

Yeah, great.
> *[The phone rings in JOSH'S darkened room.]*

You don't have a fucking answering machine?
> *[JOSH'S answering machine clicks on.]*

I was gonna say...
> *[JOSH's voice is heard on the machine, saying: "Hey,*
> *This is Josh. I'm out. You know the drill."]*

Cute.
> *[JOSH runs into his room as the machine BEEPS.]*

Uh, hey Josh, this is Ang, um, my number is—

JOSH: *[Picks up the phone.]* Yeah! Hello?

ANGIE: Um. uh. Is Josh in?

JOSH: *[Out of breath.]* This is.

ANGIE: Oh, hey Josh. ... ... This is Angie...

JOSH: *[Pause.]* Hey...

ANGIE: Hey. ...You don't sound like you want to talk to me?

JOSH: No, I uh—

ANGIE: I mean, you sound out of breath.

JOSH: ...Yeah. Yeah, I am. I just ran in. Heard the phone ringing.

ANGIE: Oh.

JOSH: Yeah.
> *[Pause.]*

Can you hold on a minute?

ANGIE: Sure.
> *[JOSH sets the phone down and goes to his closet, changing his shirt and taking off his shoes quickly. ANGIE gets up off her bed and starts pacing.]*

JOSH: *[To himself.]* Look, Angie we're obviously way past the point of no return on this one, so let's just... let's just quit while we're ahead, okay?
> *[JOSH picks up the phone, checking his hair in the mirror.]*

I'm back.
> *[Pause.]*

So...

ANGIE: How are you?

JOSH: *[Almost simultaneously.]* What have you been up to?

ANGIE: Sorry.

JOSH: *[Lays back on his bed.]* You go first.

ANGIE: Just wanted to see how you've been?

JOSH: I'm good. Going to school.

ANGIE: Yeah. How's that going? Anything interesting?

JOSH: Not really. How bout you? You still writing?

ANGIE: I'm making Thirteen-fifty an hour doing dispatch for mercy ambulance. I might go back in the fall.

JOSH: You're a good writer.

ANGIE: You only saw one essay.

JOSH: And it was very good.

ANGIE: Uh-huh.  Well I always knew what I cared about.
        *[Pause.]*
You seeing anyone?

JOSH: *[Sits up on his bed, then gets up.]*  Yeah.  ...I'm seeing someone. ... still.

ANGIE: I thought you broke up with her?

JOSH: Well ... two years is a long time.

ANGIE: Yeah, it is. Two years ago you were still telling me to keep writing.

JOSH: I guess I always tell you that.

ANGIE: Yeah.  But that's what I like about you....
        *[Silence. They both pace quietly.]*
So, you got back together with her?
        *[Pause.]*
That's good.

JOSH: So, how bout you?

ANGIE: Me?

JOSH: Yeah.

ANGIE: Oh.
        *[Pause.]*
Yeah. ... I'm seeing someone.

JOSH: What's he like?

ANGIE: He's alright. Pre-med.
> *[Silence.]*

So—

JOSH: —That's great. A career guy. How long?

ANGIE: I, uh ... six months.

JOSH: No shit. First long-termer.

ANGIE: And last. Relationships suck. Too much work.

JOSH: I thought that was a guy saying.

ANGIE: Not one of yours.

JOSH: *[Pause—that stings.]* Well we both know about me. So—

ANGIE: No. It's just—

JOSH: Mr. Marriage would never say that, would he?
> *[No response.]*

I just figured once you actually tried a relationship, you'd like it.
> *[ANGIE casually sets down her phone and walks to the
> wall that separates the rooms.]*

ANGIE: I guess I'm just not with the right guy.

JOSH: *[Pause.]* I'm sure he's cool. I'm happy for you.

ANGIE: *[Long pause.]* Thanks. So, how's your relationship going?
Everything alright?
> *[During the following exchange, ANGIE enters JOSH's
> room, comes up behind him and playfully steals his
> phone.]*

JOSH: It could be worse.

ANGIE: It could be like us.

JOSH: That'd be worse.  We'd only talk every six months.

ANGIE: I'd blow you off.

JOSH: After I pushed you away.

ANGIE: And I'd call you six months later.

JOSH: That's weird.

ANGIE: That's us. It's how we are.
> *[Silence.  ANGIE sets JOSH's phone down on his bed,*
> *takes his hand and leads him into her room.]*
It's funny.
> *[Pause.]*
You know my sister Rosa, she always says that you and I are gonna
end up together.

JOSH: Who?

ANGIE: My sister, Rosa.

JOSH: She never even met me.

ANGIE: SO!
> *[She lets go of his hand.]*
That doesn't matter.

JOSH: *[Long pause.]*  So ... what's the problem with you and your
dream guy?

ANGIE: He's not my dream guy. He's an asshole.
> *[Pause.]*
He has this ex-girlfriend in California.

JOSH: Ah.

ANGIE: Yeah.  And he went back there last month.  You know to see his friends.
> *[Pause.]*

Well, anyway... He gave me this big long explanation about how I was like this new pair of sweats—nice and new—fresh.  And she was this old, comfortable pair of sweats.  Easy to wear, you know ... comfortable. So... ...

JOSH: Sweats metaphors.

ANGIE: What do you think?

JOSH: I think you're not made of cotton.

ANGIE: I understand what he meant. ... I do.
> *[No response.]*

Well, nobody's perfect.
> *[No response.]*

Everyone can't be like you, Josh.

JOSH: *[Pause.]*  No. I guess not.

ANGIE: That's not what I meant. I mean most guys—

JOSH: Most guys don't even talk to girls who've blown them off as much as you have me. Most guys don't even get into a bizarre relationship with a girl they saw for three weeks four years ago. Especially when they already have a relationship of their own.  And most guys are much too smart to dump that girlfriend for their once-every-six-months telephone lover.
> *[JOSH turns and steps back towards his room.]*

ANGIE: Yeah.
> *[Pause.]*

What I was gonna say was that most guys don't treat girls as well as you do.
> *[He stops.]*

JOSH: Yeah. Most guys are a lot smarter than me.

ANGIE: You were smart enough to get back together with her.

JOSH: *[Pause.]* They were the only comfortable pair of sweats I had.

ANGIE: Why didn't you throw them out?
> *[ANGIE takes JOSH's hand again.]*

JOSH: There was this song ... It was on this really bad album. This George Benson  song, "Kisses in the Moonlight?"

ANGIE: I don't know it.

JOSH: You heard it.

ANGIE: No I—

JOSH: You did.
> *[He takes her hand and starts to lead her through a slow dance.]*

We danced, kissed mostly, through it.  While I was making you dinner.

ANGIE: What were you making me?

JOSH: Pasta ... My grandmother's sauce—

ANGIE: It all got stuck together—

JOSH: Because I wasn't stirring it.  I was with you, dancing...
> *[He kisses her.]*

ANGIE: I don't remember the song.

JOSH: It was really bad ...
*[He kisses her again, she responds.]*
I asked you what you thought of it, after we were done dancing.

ANGIE: Did I like it?

JOSH: You said, *[whispers]* "I didn't hear it."

ANGIE: See, that's why I didn't remember. I wasn't listening...
*[She kisses him.]*

JOSH: Must be.

ANGIE: I remember all kinds of things...

JOSH: I believe you.

ANGIE: I remember you always wanted me to watch *Star Trek* with you... I said I would try.  For you.

JOSH: We never got a chance...
*[She pulls away from him, slightly.]*

ANGIE: I remember I never apologized...

JOSH: For what?

ANGIE: I did some lousy things to you.  Said them, too...  "Mister Marriage."

JOSH: Yeah, well—

ANGIE: I'm sorry...
*[Long Pause.]*
I remember changing channels and seeing *Star Trek* on, and wanting to watch it with you.  Wanting to find out what I missed.
*[Silence.]*
So... do you think ... we'll end up together?

*[No response.]*

JOSH: *[Long Pause.]* I...
        *[ANGIE moves closer to JOSH.]*

ANGIE: Do you think we'll end up together?

JOSH: I heard you.
        *[Pause.]*
I was just thinking...

ANGIE: Of what?
        *[JOSH steps back from ANGIE.]*

JOSH: Of this *Star Trek* convention I went to a couple of years ago.

ANGIE: You're thinking of a *Star Trek* convention? A *STAR TREK* convention!?!
        *[ANGIE turns around and starts to walk away.]*

JOSH: Yeah. Shatner was there. I always wanted to see him. I grew up with Captain Kirk, so...

ANGIE: So?

JOSH: So I'm at this convention—nerds everywhere—waiting for Shatner. All the other actors had just been themselves, you know, answering questions, a joke or two. But not Shatner. He comes out onstage and starts doing this stand-up routine—one-liners and all—joke after joke. He'd answer a question, but not until he got a few jokes in. Well there was this deaf guy, a deaf mute I guess, who would hand the actors a card with his question written on it.
        *[Pause.]*
He walks up to Shatner and holds out his card. Shatner takes the card, but without even looking at it says, "I'm sorry, I don't like boys." And there's like this total silence over the convention hall. Shatner just drops the card, turns his back on the guy and goes to the other end of the stage. The guy just lets out a "Ahhhhh" or "Uhhhh" or something,

trying to ask his question. Shatner ignored him—called on someone else.

> *[Pause.]*

So the guy picked up his card and walked away.

> *[Silence. JOSH leaves her room and steps back into his own. ANGIE steps after him but stops at the invisible wall—she can't cross in.]*

It's a true story.

> *[Pause.]*

It's sick, I guess. But that show means a lot to some people. Whenever I used to watch *Star Trek,* I always thought about the future. You know, Hope. Compassion. Possibilities.

> *[JOSH picks up his phone.]*

ANGIE: That's what I always liked about you. I've been trying to watch it, you know—

JOSH: I wonder if that deaf guy thought that, too.

> *[JOSH turns his back on ANGIE holding the phone close to his ear.]*

I got a test in the morning. I gotta go.

ANGIE: *[Pause.]* Oh. *[Pause.]* You know, just because he was an asshole doesn't mean the show isn't still good. I know you know that, but—

> *[ANGIE goes to her phone and takes it in her hand.]*

JOSH: I always do have the fantasy.

ANGIE: Yeah. You always do. And—

JOSH: But the reality isn't...

> *[Pause.]*

It just isn't.

> *[ANGIE presses her phone close to her ear.]*

ANGIE: *[Long pause.]*  Well, you have your girlfriend in reality.
      *[Pause.]*
It really was great talking to you again, Josh.

JOSH: For me, too. Good luck with your boyfriend.

ANGIE: Yeah.
      *[Pause.]*
Call me sometime. Whenever.

JOSH: I will.

ANGIE: Later.
      *[They both hang up. The lights start to fade in both of
      their rooms.]*

JOSH: Yeah. ... Later.
      *[Lights out.]*


## END of PLAY

# PHONE ARTS

## LB HAMILTON

*Phone Arts* was originally produced by Poor Playwrights' Theatre at Café Copioh in Las Vegas, Nevada on April 3, 1998. The production was directed by Laura Rin. The cast was as follows:

JANE: Sheilagh Polk
MOIRE: Dawn Copeland

SETTING:
An urban apartment.

*[JANE speaks into a phone as she examines, then carefully cuts a newly baked peach pie. When she speaks, she has a syrupy Southern accent—but only when she speaks into the phone.]*

JANE: Mmmm.   It's even better than last week . . .No, I'm not lying . . . Now, why would Salome lie to you?  I swear by my baby blue eyes that Salome likes you best, Sugar. . . You are? Oooh,  I wish I could see.  Just how big is "big" Sugar?  Mmm.  I don't think I ever knew anybody ever near that—Uh huhn? Well, we'll just have to call you "Big Daddy" from now on, won't we?

*[MOIRE enters carrying an object wrapped in cloth,  she stops and takes in what JANE's doing.]*

Mmmm.  Say that again, Sugar, it makes Salome wanna eat you up, starting with your toes.... all the way up to your big, sweet—

*[MOIRE clears her throat. JANE jumps and turns.]*

Jesus!   *[beat]*  Jesus I can see it now, Sugar.  It's all you said it would be. --- Uh huhn? ....  Mmmm.  ..... Tell me, Lover. Tell me everything you do, everything...

*[MOIRE begins to flounce into the bedroom.]*

Stop!  *[To phone]*  No ... Don't stop, Sugar.  Talk to me.  *[To MOIRE]*  It's not what you think.  *[To phone.]*  It's better than you think.  God yes.  Uh huhn.  More ... don't stop.

*[MOIRE walks up to JANE and begins to speak, JANE pulls her close; gives her a very intimate kiss.  MOIRE struggles.]*

Mmmm.   Uh huhn.   More ..... Don't stop .....  *[to MOIRE]*  Stay with me, Baby.

*[MOIRE struggles. JANE hangs on and  speaks to the caller and MOIRE at the same time.]*

Don't back off now, Baby.  I have sweet peaches just for you.

*[JANE sensually slides a slice of peach into MOIRA's mouth, who surrenders, struggles and surrenders again.]*

No, don't say anything, Sugar ... just enjoy.  Mmm.  That's the sweetest stuff, Baby ... and it's all yours ... That's it!   Oh yes, oh yes, Baby.  Enjoy it....close your eyes and taste that peach ... See?  Isn't that good, Sugar?   It's all yours, 'cause little o' Salome knows how much you love my peaches.  So moist and soft and sweet and warm. Mmmm.

*[MOIRE breaks away and stomps into the bedroom. JANE
tries to follow, stretching the phone cord until it stops her
progress.]*

Damn it! *[catching herself]* Oh you're good. Come on, Baby. Come
on. I feel it. In—out, In—out, Faster baby. Faster! I want it now.
Right now....

*[A crash from the bedroom. JANE covers the phone and
whispers loudly.]*

That better not be the new marble, Moire. I'm not buying you any
more marble! *[To Phone]* That's it ... that's it! Yes, yes, oh, God, oh
God, oh God. I can't take it anymore. Stay with me, Sugar ... Stay
with me! Now ... now! NOW, damnit! Oh, Baby. Oh my. You've
just plain worn me out. . . . Sure, Honey, sure. You call again . . .
anytime. Make it soon, okay? Just make sure you all ask for
Salome, you hear? Okay, Sugar. Bye, bye. Uh huhn ... bye bye
now.... Yeah, yeah. Bye!

*[She quickly hangs up. Sound of crashes from the next room.]*

Moire? Honey? I thought you had a meeting at the gallery. Why are
you back so early? Did things go bad again? *[pause]* Look, we
need to talk. Moire, Honey? I know I said I'd quit but . . . Hell,
Moire, they're only men.

*[MOIRE finally appears from the bedroom, holding clay in
her hand.]*

MOIRE: Oh God, Jane . . . I'm so sorry. I don't know what I was
thinking. But since they're only men . . . that makes everything
different. Doesn't it—"Salome?"

*[MOIRE throws the clay at JANE and flounces back to the
bedroom.]*

JANE: I meant it's only a job!

*[MOIRE returns holding an odd shaped sculpture of a woman
straddling a large phone receiver and raises it as if to throw.]*

Sweetie? I have some Hagen Daz for the pie.

MOIRE: Why do you keep doing that?

JANE: What's wrong? Didn't Chloe like your new piece?

MOIRE: Janey answer me.

JANE: You got rejected again, didn't you, Baby?.

MOIRE: You . . ! *[beat]* Stop that. We're talking about the job.

JANE: Well, it's really more than that. You want French Vanilla, or Praline?
*[MOIRE raises the sculpture above her head in a threat.]*
Sweetie, think! That's your favorite piece. You'll only hurt yourself.

MOIRE: I have a meeting at a new gallery in exactly one-half hour, I don't have time for—

JANE: That was my birthday present!

MOIRE: You're right..
*[She puts down the sculpture and picks up the pie to throw.]*

JANE: Baby... Baby! I did what I promised. I quit 1-900-HOT TALK!
*[JANE gently takes the pie from MOIRE.]*
This is 1-900-WHISPER.

MOIRE: I think you missed the essence of our agreement.

JANE: It's my own Company, Sweetie! *[pause]* Surprised?

MOIRE: How stupid can you be?

JANE: I've made a discovery, Sweetheart and— Did you just call me stupid?

MOIRE: What happened to Wal-Mart?

JANE: Does Chloe think that I'm stu—

MOIRE: What happened to Wal-Mart, damn it!

*[The phone rings. MOIRE & JANE leap at it.]*
Hello!  *[listening]*   You want me to what? .... Uh huhn.... Uh huhn.
.... What's your name, Sir? ..... Mr. X?  Well, guess what Mr. X?
You've got the wrong number.  Salome's not going to suck your
insignificant little cock today, how do you like that?  ... What? ....
No, Mr. X,  I don't want you to beg, I want you to hang up, and then I
want you to get a goddamn life!
        *[She slams down the phone.]*
Just how much longer do you intend degrading us like this?
        *[She sets down the statue and heads to the pie and stares at it,
        then angrily takes a bite.]*

JANE: As opposed to pricing blenders and being a teeny pebble in a
great big corporate wheel, while you hang out with Chloe and all your
chic little arty friends and—

MOIRE: You're mixing metaphors again.

JANE: Well, excuse me.

MOIR: Look, Jane . . . I . . . Damnit, can we talk about this later, I've
got to get to the—

JANE: I only ever see you in bed anymore.

MOIRE: We talk.

JANE: You sleep.

MOIRE: I'm relaxing—not sleeping.

JANE: Well, you better get your sinuses checked, Honey, 'cause you
snore when you relax.

MOIRE: Do you understand what it takes for me to create?  The
energy ... the mortification of rejection—the ... I can't produce true art
in a volatile environment.

JANE: There's more to art than a lopsided hunk of clay pretending to be a woman fucking a phone.
   *[Silence. MOIRE is deeply shaken by this comment.]*

MOIRE: You're saying I have no talent?

JANE: I'm just saying, I'm finally finding out what art's really abo—

MOIRE: You might have told me seven years ago that you didn't think I have talent.

JANE: Seven years ago I hadn't spent seven years supporting your little hobby.

MOIRE: I happen to be the recipient of a Steenberg Foundation Most Promising Artist Award!

JANE: That was eight years ago.

MOIRE: Why am I'm defending my art to someone who spends her days listening to dirty old men pant?

JANE: So just how much did you make on your last sale, Darling?

MOIRE: Ah, the cruelty begins.

JANE: Mr. X's panting paid last month's rent.

MOIRE: What?

JANE: And those two-dozen long stemmed roses for our anniversary? They didn't come from Wal-mart, Lover.  1-900-WHISPER is a gold mine—much better than HOT TA—

MOIRE: Our anniversary was five months ago.
   *[The phone rings again.]*

JANE: Ummm. You never told me—Vanilla or Praline?

*[MOIRE moves to the phone, JANE picks it up then hangs it up.]*

MOIRE: You wanted to be my muse—you wanted to be the inspiration behind the—

JANE: It was love—people say crazy things when—

MOIRE: Oh God.  Last year you're begging for us to have a family and now you don't even love me?

JANE: I do want a family with you, Moire.  But—

MOIRE: And just what's Moire, Jr. going to be doing while you're jacking off Mr's. X, Y, and Z?

JANE: Why not Jane, Jr.?

MOIRE: I was being pithy.

JANE: I'm sorry. Somewhere between cleaning the oven, hand washing your undies and being stupid, I missed that word.

MOIRE: Epigrammatic.

JANE: *[beat]* Fuck you.  And fuck all your pithy friends and fuck Chloe!

MOIRE: Exactly when did this obsession with Chloe start?  *[pause]* Jane?

JANE: About ... six months ago?

MOIRE: Oh. *[beat]* Well, stop it.

JANE: About the time you started coming home late and being too tired to make love and all.

MOIRE: I explained that . . .

JANE: About the time I saw you and the Divine Chloe about to dive for oysters in your studio. *[silence]* Yeah. Right then I asked myself, how the hell does a Jane compete with a Chloe?

MOIRE: It was . . . I . . . Look, nothing really happened. You misunderstoo—

JANE: And Jane couldn't. Not really. 'Cause Jane's just a regular type person, right?

MOIRE: Chloe wanted to . . . well ... but I couldn't . . .

JANE: And I'm thinking, Chloe's got the clothes, and the body, and the connections, right?

MOIRE: One stupid, heated moment, Jane. That's all.

JANE: So one day, I'm baking myself sick, and I'm looking at this statue here. Thinking about Wal-Mart and the seven-year itch and how good Chloe looks in her size 2 black dresses and her pouty lips. Suddenly the statue starts speaking to me and—like I finally begin to understand, you know? Communication, art, passion, it's all mixed up together, right? That's what Chloe and Moire have that Jane and Moire don't have. And that's when it hits—the statue—the phone— my voice—talent! I have a talent too! I can be creative!

MOIRE: I realize you were hurt by what you thought you saw, but ...

JANE: Yeah, yeah. Anyway, then the power . . . the power of art finally begins to make sense.

MOIRE: The pain you must have felt . . . I'll never forgive myself.

JANE: It's fine, Moire. Chloe gave you what I couldn't. But now ... now we finally have something in common.

MOIRE: Jane!  It's over.  Long over.

JANE: Long over?

MOIRE: I'm a one woman, woman.

JANE: Oh…

MOIRE: Sweetheart.  I just can't do that to you.

JANE: Oh?

MOIRE: Come here.  Come here, Silly.  Look at me.  Is this the face of an adulteress?  Is it?  No.  All better?  Promise?  That's my girl. Now call the damn phone company, or whoever and stop this craziness.  Okay?  *[pause]*  What's the matter?

JANE: I can't.  Listen, Moire . . . I'm good.  I found my path.  I am a performance artist!

MOIRE: *[beat]*  Where's the Hagen Daz?

JANE: I have instincts, Sweetie.  And a following.  I know what they need even when they don't.  I can talk whole new worlds for them and take them where they never knew they could go.  I can make them laugh; I can make them cry; and they are in a big new place and are ... are ... transformed.  And they come back for more—it's a built-in market with huge return business!  And they don't have to dress up and go somewhere and hang out with a bunch of snooty strangers to find art—No ... it's right there, at their fingertips.  And my art can't be stolen from them and it won't be ruined by time, or lose value, because mine is a living art—always ... always ... um ... reinventing itself!  Yeah!  Powerful and, and ... um ... and empowering!

MOIRE: That's not art—

JANE: Of course it is.  In your face, real ... um ... audiophonic!  Yeah! Audiophonic art.  Oh think about it, Sweetie.  We could branch out.

Make a fortune, buy a house—have that baby?   AND you won't have
to worry about critics!

MOIRE: Me?  Oh, no!  Uhn uhn!

JANE: Sweetie.  I need you.  You're my muse, now!  *[pause]*  Wow,
my shift's just about up.  I've got to meet with my accountant.  Do
you think you can throw something together for dinner?

MOIRE: I don't cook.

JANE: We have three cookbooks, you'll be fine.  *[Kissing MOIRE]*
Thanks.  Thanks for opening all those doors for me, Love.
        *[ She gathers her things.  The phone rings.  MOIRE stares at
        it.]*
Answer it, Sweetie.

MOIRE: I . . . it's—it's perverted.

JANE: It's Postmodern!   Go on . . . you can do it.  *[Beat]*  Please?
*[beat]*  For me?  *[beat]*  For the baby?
        *[MOIRE struggles, then gingerly picks up the phone.  JANE
        cuddles close to listen and whisper instructions.]*

MOIRE: Hello?....  What?  Oh . . . uh, this is . . . my name is—
Peaches.  *[listens]*  What?!
        *[She covers the phone and whispers.]*
I can't do this.
        *[JANE nods encouragement and starts nibbling MOIRE's
        neck.]*
Mmm.  Uh, sure . . . I'm alone.  Uh, so . . . ummm.
        *[JANE whispers in MOIRE's ear and pushes her into a chair.]*
Tell me . . . what are you wearing?
        *[JANE begins to stroke MOIRE's breast.]*
Ohhh, I like that . . . Uh huhn.
        *[The women smile at each other and JANE begins to sink to
        her knees.]*
Tell me more.  Lot's more.

*[She continues to moan as the Lights Fade.]*

\* \* \*

# FUGUE

LAURA ELIZABETH MILLER

*Fugue* was originally produced in October 2004 at Texas Wesleyan University in Fort Worth, Texas. The production was directed by Jessica Roberts. The cast was as follows:

AMY: Jaad Saxton
GLADYCE: Shay Dial
LIZZIE: Michelle Cahill
HARRY: Eric Briggs

**fugue**; noun
1. a: a musical composition in which one or two themes are repeated or imitated by successively entering voices and contrapuntally developed in a continuous interweaving of the voice parts
   b: something that resembles a fugue especially in interweaving repetitive elements
2. a disturbed state of consciousness in which the one affected seems to perform acts in full awareness but upon recovery cannot recollect the deeds

*[As the lights rise AMY can be seen twirling slowly, enjoying the swish of her skirt. LIZZY plays with a doll and GLADYCE reads a book. HARRY watches.]*

AMY: When I was eight, I was murdered.

LIZZY: I was only seven.

GLADYCE: I was ten and should have known better.

AMY: I was wearing my favorite blue dress.

LIZZY: And playing with Disco Barbie!

GLADYCE: I was reading Nancy Drew.

AMY: I didn't know it then.

GLADYCE: I later found out—

AMY: He was watching me from his window.

GLADYCE: For days he watched me from his window.

AMY: Sitting in his yellow chair.

LIZZY: He sat in an old yellow chair. And he had a kitty on his knee.

AMY: One foot pressing against the floor.

GLADYCE: Rocking.

LIZZY: Rocking.

AMY: But before he started watching—

GLADYCE: I found out later before he started watching—

AMY: He dug lots of little holes.

LIZZY: Holes and holes and holes!

GLADYCE: He dug hundreds of holes.

AMY: Under the house.

GLADYCE: In Mrs. Stuart's flowerbed where he saw his cat take a shit.

LIZZY: Around the roots of my daddy's pecan tree!

AMY: And in these holes—

GLADYCE: One little piece at a time—

AMY: He buried me.

LIZZY: And me.

AMY: First my hands.

GLADYCE: Then my neck. I didn't know you could separate the head from the neck and the neck from the shoulders.

AMY: But you can.

GLADYCE: He buried me and forgot.

AMY: He buried me and forgot.

LIZZY: And me.

AMY: But first—
    *[The girls scatter to their original positions. One girl twirling. One girl playing with her doll. The other reading.]*

HARRY: Hello, Amy.

AMY: Hello.

HARRY: Hello, Lizzy.

LIZZY: Hi.

HARRY: I'm Harry. Isn't your name Gladyce? I'm a friend of your mom's.

GLADYCE: I've never seen you before.

HARRY: I'm an old friend.

GLADYCE: What's her name then?

HARRY: Julie.

AMY: Well, bye now.

HARRY: Where are you going Amy?

AMY: I wasn't going to say anymore.

GLADYCE: I was going to run.

LIZZY: But then Harry said—

HARRY: I have some kittens. I found them. They're in a box in my garage. Would you like to see them? You can take one home if you want to.

LIZZY: Kitties?

HARRY: That's right.

LIZZY: Really?

HARRY: I found some kittens. They're in my garage. There's four of them. Would you like to see them?

AMY: What color are they?

HARRY: One is white. Another is an orange tabby. My favorite is the black one. Do you want me to show you?

GLADYCE: I don't think my mom would like me talking to you. I need to go home.

AMY: I should have gone home.

LIZZY: I didn't think of going home.

HARRY: She said it would be okay if you came over. I could show you my parakeet.

GLADYCE: When did you talk to her?

HARRY: I called her this afternoon. She said you could come over and see my pets because you love animals. You love animals, don't you?

AMY: Yes! I sure do! I have a dog. His name is Chew Toy!

HARRY: I know. He's a big black dog.

LIZZY: He's a lab! You've seen him? Out your window?

HARRY: I sure have.

GLADYCE: I don't have a dog. And I thought you had a cat. Not a bird.

AMY: When did you call my mom?

HARRY: Today.

AMY: While she was at work?

HARRY: That's right.

LIZZY: You called my mom?

HARRY: I found her number in the phone book.

LIZZY: Okay.

AMY: He took my hand.

GLADYCE: He was wearing gloves.

LIZZY: He had on funny gloves.

GLADYCE: They were made of rubber.

LIZZY: But they weren't yellow like mommy's. They were black.

GLADYCE: Up here—

AMY: From up here—

GLADYCE: You see a lot from this view.

AMY: You see a lot that you can't see when you're below.

GLADYCE: He was smiling.

AMY: And I don't know why, but—

GLADYCE: I felt a little sick inside.

LIZZY: Let's go see the kitties, can we?

HARRY: Of course. Here. Hold my hand.

LIZZY: Why are you wearing gloves?

GLADYCE: It wasn't cold.

AMY: It was warm.

HARRY: Because my hands get cold.

LIZZY: Oh.

AMY: But somehow kitties made up for everything.

GLADYCE: Kitties made me curious.

LIZZY: Kitties!

AMY: I thought, maybe, just for a second...

GLADYCE: I thought I would leave, after a minute.

LIZZY: I wanted to go. He had kitties.

GLADYCE: Why do you have dirt on your knees?

HARRY: I've been working in my garden.

LIZZY: Your knees are really dirty.

HARRY: I've been digging.

AMY: What for?

HARRY: It's like a little grave.

LIZZY: Did something die?

HARRY: Yes.

GLADYCE: I should have run. I might—

AMY: If only I had run—

GLADYCE: Instead—

LIZZY: A kitty?

HARRY: I think it was sick. Do you still want to see the others?

GLADYCE: Are they sick too?

AMY: The cats are sick?

HARRY: No. I don't think so.

GLADYCE: Why was I so concerned about cats?

AMY: Well, okay. I want to see them.

GLADYCE: Never mind. I don't want to see them.

AMY: We walked on the sidewalk together. He held my hand and gave me a piece of candy.

LIZZY: He gave me candy and we were friends.

GLADYCE: I tried to walk away but—

AMY: He started squeezing my hand.

LIZZY: He petted the top of my head like this!

GLADYCE: Let me go!

HARRY: This is my house.

AMY: You live really close to me.

HARRY: Let's go inside.

AMY: My tummy twisted.

GLADYCE: Intuition.

LIZZY: You said the kitties were in the garage.

HARRY: I made a little coffin for the one that died. It's in my kitchen.

AMY: Intuition.

LIZZY: I'm scared.

GLADYCE: Stomach twisting.

AMY: I think I should go home.

HARRY: Help me bury her.

LIZZY: No! I wanna go home.

HARRY: Alright. I'll bury her later. Let's go to the garage.

AMY: It was a girl?

HARRY: Yes. A little girl. Are you sure you don't want to see her?

LIZZY: I'm sure.

AMY: He grabbed my hand.

GLADYCE: He dragged me around the corner.

AMY: I tried to walk faster to keep up.

LIZZY: Wait for me.

HARRY: Here, you go in first. I'll turn on the light.

LIZZY: I'm scared of the dark.

AMY: Where are they?

HARRY: In the corner. Can't you hear them crying?

AMY: There was nothing.

GLADYCE: Just my heart pounding in my ears.

LIZZY: Kitty? Kitty?

AMY: A light snapped on.

GLADYCE: I was blinded.

LIZZY: I can't see!

AMY: I turned—

LIZZY: He held me tight.

GLADYCE: He slapped me across the face.

AMY: The brass chain from the light bulb danced above his head.

GLADYCE: The brass chain from the light bulb danced above his head.

LIZZY: Look at the chain dance!

AMY: Too late.

GLADYCE: I was too late.

LIZZY: He pushed me down.

AMY: I don't want to see them!

LIZZY: Mommy!

GLADYCE: Mama!

AMY: He pushed me into the wall.

LIZZY: I want my—

GLADYCE: He hit me again.

AMY: I couldn't move.

LIZZY: Stop! Please!

GLADYCE: I saw a flash.

AMY: Something flashed.

LIZZY: I saw silver.

GLADYCE: Oh my God!

AMY: Please God!

GLADYCE: A knife.

AMY: A blade.

LIZZY: What are you doing?

GLADYCE: I'm dying.

AMY: I'm dying.

HARRY: Close your eyes.

LIZZY: Why?

HARRY: So it won't hurt.

AMY: And it was over.

GLADYCE: It came so quick.

AMY: He kissed me.

GLADYCE: Then he put the knife here.

AMY: Here.

LIZZY: Here.

AMY: I was gone.

GLADYCE: Gone.

LIZZY: Gone?

HARRY: Yes.

AMY: I was so small.

GLADYCE: I never realized how little I was.

LIZZY: Look. A little girl. It's me.

AMY: It is you.

GLADYCE: I'm Gladyce. This is Amy.

LIZZY: My name is Lizzy.

AMY: Hold my hand.

LIZZY: Why is he kissing me?

AMY: I think he's saying goodbye.

GLADYCE: He kissed my nose.

AMY: My lips.

LIZZY: What will he do with me?

GLADYCE: He buried my knees next to my mother's front step.  He did it in the middle of the night.

AMY: He'll put you away.

LIZZY: In little holes?

AMY: In little holes.

GLADYCE: In damned little holes!

AMY: Then he will forget.

GLADYCE: He will forget.

LIZZY: His memory is broken?

AMY: He'll look out his window.

GLADYCE: He'll forget and look out his window.

LIZZY: Out his window…

AMY: Again.


END